THE CARTEL QUEEN

A Scott Stiletto Thriller 9

BRIAN DRAKE

WOLFPACK
PUBLISHING
— EST 2013 —

The Cartel Queen
(Scott Stiletto 9)
Brian Drake

Wolfpack Publishing
5130 S. Fort Apache Rd. 215-380
Las Vegas, NV 89148

Paperback Edition
Copyright © 2022 Brian Drake

Paperback ISBN 978-1-63977-978-9
eBook ISBN 978-1-63977-977-2
LCCN 2022939646

THE CARTEL QUEEN

CHAPTER ONE

The Past

There were advantages to being a government killer. One knew how to make the hit and get away. Scott Stiletto had invented a few tricks exclusive to his own killing skills. He was one of the best for a reason. Tonight, he'd put his skills to use to avenge the death of somebody close to him.

The drug pushers who worked the east side of the city met once a week in the basement of an abandoned building. The top dog of the outfit had purchased the downtown structure for his base of operations. The fence around the property, and the gutted cement and steel frames, remained a fixed point on the downtown street corner. It was an eyesore amidst the other buildings in the area, all of which had undergone extensive remodeling and upgrades to bring "new life" into the downtown sector. As for the one building which remained untouched, there was nothing the neighbors could do. They speculated and gossiped about why the building owner continued to fail to get his act together and get the place open for business.

If they only knew what really went on in the bowels of the building.

Scott Stiletto watched from the top of a parking garage across the street. The stoplight at the intersection he faced cast a red, yellow, and green glow over his spot as it cycled, but there was no traffic to meter at this hour of the night.

The drug runners arrived on foot over a thirty-minute period. They arrived alone or in pairs and slipped through an opening in the fence. Through a night-vision headset, Stiletto tracked their movement. They followed a walkway to a steel door. Stiletto had no view of the steel door from his position, but he knew it was there from his recon the night before. The recon had shown him what lay beyond the door as well, and he'd inspected the "kill zone" in detail. A stairwell to the basement. It wasn't one room, but the start of many rooms for building infrastructure and maintenance. A second entry was on the opposite side of the building, a half block away, in the underground garage.

Stiletto counted the drug runners as they arrived. Then ten minutes of no new arrivals passed. Two more needed to show up before the meeting began. They were the two he wanted most.

He was on his own; this mission was personal. He was a junior officer with CIA covert ops, but officially on leave to help with a family emergency. His niece, Bailey Rose, was dead from a drug overdose. Scott had helped his brother bury the teenager two weeks ago. He remained with the family to provide emotional support, but he had a second agenda as well. Kill the people responsible. Only then could he return to Langley and resume official duties. If his boss at the CIA, General Ike Fleming, had any indication what Stiletto was actually staying behind to do, he'd given no sign when granting the extra time off.

There he is. Stiletto watched the straggler slip through the fence. This one differed from the others. He carried two heavy tote bags. Totes full of fresh narcotics to distribute to the pushers. One more to go, and it was shooting time.

Scott had come prepared, but took the attitude of a submarine commander, despite his dislike for being on water. Run silent, run deep. He'd rigged his weapons for near-silent operation.

The Colt Combat Government pistol, customized to his own specifications, rode under his left arm with an extended tube attached to the barrel. The suppressor would reduce the subsonic .45 ACP ammunition to a thump and click of the gun's action.

His own tote bag contained other tools. Tear gas grenades. Filter mask. A Heckler & Koch MP5SD3 with integral suppressor. The opposition's guns had no such capability; as long as the fight stayed below ground, Scott wasn't worried about the noise. But he was one against many. The fight had a good chance of spilling onto the street if he wasn't careful. The goal was to prevent any of them from getting away.

There were no civilians to worry about. The city blocks were corporate offices, and businesses catering to the office trade. All were closed, dark, empty. From his period of surveillance, Scott knew the local cops did not prowl through unless an alarm went off in one of the buildings. There were overnight security guards in most of the offices, but if they heard any shooting, they'd hide and call 9-1-1. It was the only variable he couldn't overcome. The fight had to stay below the street. He'd only follow a quarry to the surface if forced. He had no intention of extending his stay; the drug gang died *now*. They would never see the sun again.

Stiletto's pulse quickened as the last man arrived. The boss. The man who'd collect his take from the pushers and issue new instructions. Stiletto watched him through the night vision goggles. Dark mop of hair. Short and bulging in the middle. He glanced around before slipping through the fence, then went through the door to the basement.

Killing time.

Stiletto stowed the NVGs in the tote, slung the bag cross-body, and left the roof. He took his time on the stairs to the street. He didn't need a slip-and-fall and resulting broken ankle to derail his mission.

He'd been with the CIA for two years as a Ground Branch operative for Special Activities. His normal duties consisted of counter-terrorist operations and training indigenous personnel in the Middle East. But he'd learned the fighting arts in the army. Airborne. Special Forces. Every high-speed low-drag op the brass cooked up. He'd retired from the army with the rank of major. Years of going where ordered, fighting for his country. Tonight, he commanded himself.

This one's for me.

Stiletto reached the sidewalk and paused in a dark alcove. There was a freeway overpass two miles south of him. He only heard the low drone of fast-moving cars.

He let two minutes tick by before crossing the street. He hurried across the intersection to the abandoned building.

———

Zac Pope slipped through the gap in the fence. The front of his shirt caught on one of the broken chain links thanks to the bowling ball belly under the garment. Zac pulled the fabric free with a curse. *Fat ass. Christ, eat a salad sometimes.*

He followed a concrete path as it started toward a door at the end, flanked on either side by concrete slabs to create a narrow walk space. He opened the door. The hinges squeaked. If his men were in the middle of a bull session, they'd shut up at the sound of the hinges and wait for Zac's arrival. If not, he'd shout until they calmed down and paid attention to him.

Zac turned left as the door closed with a thud. He advanced down the steps to a narrow hall with only a single bulb in the ceiling lighting the way. At the end of the hall, an open doorway fed into the main where the crew met for meetings.

"The Holy Father is here," announced his second-in-command, Ruben Cortez. Zac frowned. He hated the nickname but found no way to argue—his last name was Pope. Short of shooting Cortez, he wasn't sure how to make him stop. At least Cortez didn't call him Fat Fuck. If anybody did, it was behind his back.

He figured his crew could use the name to blow off steam whenever he climbed their asses, like he planned to do tonight. As long as he didn't know, he didn't care.

"All right, listen up," Zac shouted. His men quieted

down. They sat on folding chairs in three rows. He stood in front of them. The only member of the crew not seated was Apollo Short. The tall black man leaned against the wall with his two tote bags at his feet and his arms folded. He appeared bored.

Zac stepped in front of the seated hustlers. He said, "We got some heat on us. Hey, Snake. Yeah, you. One of your high school girls crashed and burned."

"No shit?"

"She died too. My people at Division Eight are looking for you. Maybe stay away from East Side High for a bit."

"East Side gonna get high," said another pusher, to a chorus of giggles and snorts.

"Quiet," Zac snapped. The laugher ceased. "Anybody gets picked up, you have one job. Shut your goddamn mouth. Do not talk to the cops. Mr. Lowenstein can get you out within twenty-four hours if you keep your fucking mouth shut. No tryin' to fool the cops with your bullshit. Get it? There won't be any trouble if you keep your dick holster closed."

The crew got it and said so. Zac scoffed. He had to repeat the statement several times because he knew one of his idiots would talk too much and put them all at risk. They all thought they were smarter than the cops when most hadn't finished high school.

"Okay, Apollo, you're up. Pass out the new shit. Everybody gives Apollo their money and don't hold nothin' back or it's yo' big dumb ass."

Apollo pushed way from the wall and grabbed one of the totes. As he pulled the zipper, an object clattered into the room, rolling across the floor. Somebody shouted, "What the—" but then nobody else talked. They started screaming instead. The canister on the floor popped and hissed white smoke. Tear gas. Even Zac Pope felt the effects right away. His eyes stung and he choked. And then somebody entered with a machine gun and started blasting.

————

Stiletto eased through the broken fence. He pushed the gap open wider to accommodate his tote. Guiding the gap closed by hand, he turned for the cement path and followed it to the door.

He knew the hinges made noise so he'd come prepared.

Run silent, run deep.

From the tote he grabbed a can of WD-40 and sprayed a large amount of the lubricant on each hinge. He put the can back and took out his gas mask. While the WD-40 penetrated the rotating points of each hinge, he donned the mask, confirmed the rubber seal was tight against his smooth skin, and reached into the tote for the MP5SD3 submachine gun.

The mask covered most of his face and eyes, the twin filters protruding on either side of his cheeks. He opened the door. No noise. No sentry, either. Zac Pope thought his gang was totally safe at such an hour. He was about to learn having cops on the payroll didn't promise safety of any kind.

Down the steps. Into the hall. Light bulb in the ceiling. Voices. The meeting was underway. Scott paused to take a tear gas grenade from his tote. He pulled the pin and rolled the canister ahead like a bowling ball. The canister bounced and clattered and entered the room.

"What the—" *Pop. Hissssss.* Yelling and screaming followed. The white cloud filled the room. With no open windows, no windows at all, actually, the gas hung below the ceiling.

Stiletto braced in the doorway and opened fire with the HK. A swarm of suppressed nine-millimeter death spit from the muzzle. Men already screaming from the gas now screamed for another reason. *Pain.* A fire of pain as bullets ripped through their bodies.

The drug gang fell out of their chairs, stumbling, falling. Some fell for good. Others survived the first salvo but Stiletto wasn't done. He swapped the empty magazine for a full one and left the doorway. The HK whispered some more, singing its murder song, accompanied by a chorus of yells cut short, bodies slapping concrete as they fell.

Stiletto ran the HK empty again and pulled the Colt .45. A man by the wall crawled on hands and knees— Apollo Short, the supplier. Stiletto walked by and shot him in the back of the head. The pusher's body flopped and stopped moving.

The last two at the front of the room also lay on the floor, gasping, teary-eyed, saliva and snot running down their faces. Stiletto put a bullet through Ruben Cortez's left eye as the second-in-command lifted his head to try and comprehend the masked wraith above him.

Scott turned the Colt on Zac Pope. The leader tried to wipe his face and talk but only uttered garbled gibberish. The .45 spoke again. The slug carved a tunnel through Zac's brain. He fell face first onto the ground and lay still.

Stiletto stowed the pistol and stepped over bodies on his way out. The fresh air felt welcome when he tore off the mask. A hurried two-block trot to his car and he put the slaughter zone behind him. Mission accomplished.

He drove with his jaw clenched. A bunch of dead

druggies didn't bring Bailey Rose back, and he'd done nothing to stop the flow of narcotics into the city. But he found solace in vengeance. Minor vengeance, perhaps. Cartel involvement in the financing of terrorism meant he'd fight the source soon enough as part of his work at CIA. And he looked forward to the fight.

CHAPTER TWO

The Present

Stiletto's days in the CIA were far behind him. He worked for a private organization called The Trust now, and he once again found himself where he most thrived. Combat.

Albeit quiet combat, so far.

"Here's your gin and tonic," the young lady said.

Stiletto accepted the drink with a smile and thanked the lady. She didn't look like she was over twenty-five. Long black hair, plump in her tight-fitting cocktail dress with a too-short skirt, her black-framed glasses giving her a "hot nerd" look. The lights above reflected off her lenses as she turned to the man seated next to Scott. The other customer had trouble keeping his eyes off her. Even Scott had to remind himself to look in her eyes and not stare or let his gaze linger elsewhere. She pivoted and carried her now empty tray away.

Stiletto and the other man sat on soft chairs in a back

corner of the hotel lounge in Washington, DC. A small table sat in front of them. They had to lean forward to reach the table, so Scott held onto his drink after taking a sip. He watched his companion place his glass on the table.

Warren Hardison was toned and chiseled with dark stubble on his jaw. Black hair, slicked back, fingers decorated with shiny rings. He wore black. A leather carrying case rested beside his chair. Scott's objective was to get the item inside the case. A briefcase full of marked money waited at his feet to facilitate the exchange.

Hardison said, "Congratulations on the winning bid."

They'd made small talk while waiting for the drinks. Scott was glad to finally talk business.

"You drive a hard bargain, Mr. Hardison."

"The name fits, eh?" He smiled with perfect teeth. "May I see the money?"

Stiletto placed his drink on the table. His blazer fell open, but if Hardison spotted the .45 in the speed rig under his left arm, Stiletto didn't mind. The other man may not have been unarmed, but he had security close. Two men in gray suits, Hardison's people, sat in another corner watching the meeting.

Scott picked up the briefcase and handed it to Hardison. The seller placed the case on his lap and popped the locks. Lifting the lid high enough to peek inside, he whistled. He didn't see Stiletto slip a finger under the left cuff of his blazer and press a button on his watch.

Hardison closed the case and gestured toward his security. One of the men came over and took the case. The man carried the case to a back room.

"Hey—" Stiletto began.

"We have to count it," Hardison said. "I'm sure you

understand. We can't flash that much money around here, get it?"

"Let's see what I'm buying."

Hardison smiled again and opened his own bag. He pulled out a laptop. Scott grabbed his drink to make room on the table. Hardison turned on the computer. While it booted, he extracted another item from the bag. Stiletto watched with interest.

The second item was a sophisticated piece of electronic gear. A short cable extended from the back. Buttons on the front. A stainless steel casing protected the electrical circuits within.

Hardison plugged the unit into the laptop's USB and pushed a button. Red and green lights came to life. He logged into the laptop and selected a program from the desktop display. He tapped the mouse pad twice.

Stiletto sipped his drink and watched. His backup crew would be in position by now. He sat with a steady pulse and appeared bored. He felt the eyes of Hardison's remaining "security man" on him. The goon was a shooter. He might have been wearing a fancy suit, but the bulge under the coat betrayed the pistol concealed under his left arm.

The laptop screen came to life as the selected program loaded. An animated outline of the globe rotated in the center of the screen. Red and green dots encircled the globe in a random pattern.

"There you are," Hardison said. He swallowed more of his Johnny Walker. The ice cubes in the glass clinked. "Current positions of US military and spy satellites. You can monitor their orbit in real time. Your clients will know when one passes over their area, and they'll have time to hide and cover any equipment or personnel they don't want the prying eyes of the CIA to see."

"Amazing," Stiletto said. He turned the laptop toward him for a better look. "How did you do it?"

Hardison chuckled. "Hacker's secret. Of course, if the money is the correct amount, you'll get everything, including technical support for six months. And you'll be talking to me, nobody else."

Hardison's device could not fall into the wrong hands. The Trust had worked hard and bid high for the device, beating every other bidder, including the CIA. Stiletto laughed when the Agency he'd once worked for refused to go higher and decided on direct action instead. Hardison had been one step ahead of them and slipped through the dragnet, but now The Trust had him dead bang. All Stiletto had to do was close the deal and let the backup team do the tough part. The Trust wanted Hardison alive. They wanted the secrets locked away in his mind.

"Where's your man?" Stiletto said.

On cue, the gunner Hardison had sent to count the money returned. He handed the briefcase to his boss. The man said, "All there. Two million, non-sequential, used bills."

Stiletto said, "As agreed."

Hardison placed the briefcase on the floor. He quickly closed the laptop, unplugged the tracking device, and stowed them in the bag. Stiletto frowned as the second goon joined them.

"Our terms have changed," Hardison announced. He rose and picked up both the leather bag and briefcase. "The price is now four million and thank you for the down payment. We will be in touch."

"You can't change the deal."

"Unless you want an incident here at this nice hotel,

you'll stay in your seat. Do not reach under your coat. I'm leaving Robert here to watch you."

Hardison and the man who counted the money departed. The remaining gunner took Hardison's chair. The man extracted a wallet and placed two $20 bills on the table.

He said in a gravelly voice, "Can't leave without paying for the drinks, right?"

Stiletto gave him a smile. He kept his arms on the chair's armrests. Hardison and his goon would be heading for their chosen exit and Scott figured it wasn't the front door. Didn't matter. He was walking straight into the backup team.

He glanced around. Other patrons sat at the bar. Some occupied tables. He didn't want anybody hurt in a crossfire. *Dammit!*

"Sit tight," the gunner named Robert said. "Only a few more minutes."

"You aren't kidding."

"Hmmm?"

"More like a few more seconds."

The impact of the words made the goon's face change. He realized Stiletto had a plan of his own and reached for his gun.

Shouts erupted. *"Freeze! Stop right there!"* A gun went off. The crack of the shot echoed through the lobby, an ear-piercing *bang* indicating sudden and deadly violence. The lounge patrons reacted with surprise, gasps, shouts of fright.

The goon jumped to his feet and drew his gun, but he was too close to Stiletto. Scott kicked him in the left knee. The big man yelped and stumbled. He didn't fall. He leveled his gun and Stiletto stood in a flash of speed.

He punched the man in the jaw, then grabbed the table, and smashed the hard wood over the man's head.

Stiletto ran with the .45 in hand. "Everybody get down!"

Chaos filled the lobby. Near a side exit, members of Stiletto's team kicked the gun away from Hardison's fallen shooter. The man lay in a pool of blood. His boss, still clutching both cases, was running across the lobby for the front entrance.

Stiletto sprinted after the hacker, shouting his name, the Colt .45 tight in his right fist. Hardison snapped a glance over his shoulder. As he faced forward again, he slipped on the smooth tile. His sprint slowed. Stiletto reached him and smashed the barrel of the Colt over Hardison's head. The hacker dropped like a sack of grain.

"It's all right!" Scott shouted. He stowed his gun and bent over to grab the cases. Two members of his team took charge of Hardison. One cuffed his arms behind his back. They lifted the unconscious man to his feet.

As the witnesses calmed down, Stiletto added a final touch.

"We're FBI, it's okay!" he shouted.

A lie was better than the truth they couldn't say in a case like this one, he decided. But the dead gunner might pose a problem.

CHAPTER THREE

At the corner of a busy intersection in Washington, DC, a nondescript single-level gray building stood anonymously. Blacked-out windows, the exterior paint faded, the walls pock-marked. A perpetual For Lease sign hung on one side facing the busy street, but anybody calling the number to inquire about the lease received a message saying the line had been disconnected.

Nothing about the building stood out unless a passerby wondered why such a run-down place remained standing. Most pedestrians paid it no attention. It was a familiar sight and thus invisible. Anybody breaching the exterior would find only an empty interior, the floor covered with debris, and no sign of use. But beneath the building was where the secrets of the abandoned building lay.

Under the street lurked the Washington, DC, headquarters of The Trust. The small complex consisted of what the daily crew called the Pit, a cluster of computer workstations with large monitors on the walls. To either side of the Pit were offices and conference rooms. The

Pit was where the crew provided support and real-time intelligence for field operatives while also collecting and analyzing incoming information.

The Trust wasn't an official apparatus of any nation's intelligence community. It was a group run by former intelligence officers who wanted to continue the fight and keep disaster at bay but avoid governmental interference and red tape.

Stiletto followed the underground tunnel from the parking garage across the street, and entered HQ within an hour after the Hardison episode at the hotel. The backup team had transported Hardison to an interrogation center outside the city, and Scott needed to follow up with his boss. He found General Isaac Fleming in his office off the Pit.

General Fleming had been Scott's chief at CIA, too, until political shenanigans forced him out via firing. Since reuniting with Scott at The Trust, the two carried on like old times. Both held a small level of animosity toward the CIA, and Fleming allowed his to display itself as he faced Stiletto from across his desk.

"What's better?" Fleming said. "That the CIA failed to secure the Hardison device, or we didn't?"

"Bragging rights all around for sure, sir," Stiletto said. "And the FBI cover held, by the way."

"Good. They'll know it was us soon enough. It feels good to eat the FBI's lunch too."

Stiletto agreed. While he had been fired from the CIA over an unauthorized mission, and, frankly, had deserved his fate, the new regime at CIA had forced Fleming out because he wasn't part of their club. They had an official excuse, of course. Fleming was old. Tired. Not up to the task any longer, they said. He'd made too many mistakes, mistakes enabled by traitors within the organization later rooted out by Scott. He knew bullshit when he heard it. The General was as sharp as ever. The Trust took him aboard and for better pay too.

General Ike, as he was known, had retired from the army before assuming leadership with the CIA covert operations division. He might have been ex-army, but he decorated his office with paintings of 18th Century naval vessels. The days of wooden ships and iron men. He wanted to extend the philosophy to his own people. It was a myth, sure. People were people, flesh and blood and fallible. But those men had faced many of the same difficulties as the General and his crew hundreds of years later, but they had something in common despite the distance of time. They had to overcome the obstacles with strength and determination. The enemy was not allowed to win.

They discussed the Hardison situation further. If the hacker hadn't pulled his double cross, there wouldn't have been a shooting. The General was glad they kept the exchange of gunfire to the bare minimum necessary.

"What happens to Hardison now?" Stiletto asked.

"He'll be interrogated. We'll find out how many other systems he's hacked. Once FBI and CIA find out we have him, I'm sure we'll have an argument over who gets to keep him. We'll hang onto Hardison as long as we can, and, heck, if we offer him a deal to work for us in the end, the CIA can go choke."

Stiletto smiled. "Right on, sir."

"Anyway, good work. I know it wasn't easy."

"Will there be anything more today, General?"

"You got a date or something?"

"No, sir, the therapist you recommended. My appointment is in two hours."

"Busy day for you."

"Yes, sir."

"I think Dr. Gargarin will be good for you."

Stiletto didn't want to admit work and life was beginning to be too much to juggle. After a period of depression a two-week fishing trip failed to cure, Scott told the boss he needed help. Fleming suggested a therapist who counseled many in the intelligence community. He could trust Dr. Gargarin to keep his mouth shut and provide a sympathetic ear.

Stiletto's issues went deep, though. One visit wasn't going to fix much. But it was a start.

CHAPTER FOUR

Stiletto said, "I'm not used to talking about my problems, doctor."

The therapist maintained a stoic face. He sat with crossed legs, notepad on his lap. He might have been a history professor based on his attire. Tweed jacket, rumpled shirt and slacks. Gray hair, bald patch on top. A living stereotype. But General Fleming had promised Dr. Joseph Gargarin was the man to see, so he swept aside the negative thoughts.

"Then why are you here?" Gargarin said.

"Because not talking about my problems is becoming a problem."

Gargarin laughed. "Here I am. Start with your background, if you don't mind."

"You have my file."

"I do. But hard facts don't tell me anything *real* about you."

Stiletto had refused the couch. He sat in a soft leather chair near the couch, since he had no interest in being a stereotype himself. Or maybe he was the other stereotype who refused to be a stereotype. *You're thinking too much*, he thought. *You're trying to be smart but all you are is nervous. It's okay to feel nervous.*

The days of an intelligence officer feeling ashamed of talking about problems had long passed. In the old days, alcohol was a solution; until too many alcoholics resulted, and the bosses at CIA needed a solution to all the drunks at Company desks. Drinking was discouraged through the usual public service campaigns and changes in societal behavior; drinking lessened, but problems remained unsolved. Stiletto often joked alcohol probably did help *mute* problems, which was *almost* as good as solving them, but saying so always stirred up the "health conscious" into explaining why he was wrong. Eventually doctors like Joseph Gargarin became as much a part of the intelligence community as the everyday analyst, and the resistance to seeing such doctors faded. Some never hesitated to attend a confidential therapy session, but they also never spoke about doing so. Stiletto didn't plan to broadcast he was seeing Doctor Gargarin, but if the topic ever came up, he wouldn't shy away. Nobody would insult him. And somebody might ask for a referral. There was no shame in admitting you needed help.

The end table between the couch and chair contained a plastic flower in a pot and a box of tissues. Stiletto might need the tissues if the conversation turned rough, which he expected. Life had not been easy the last few years. He had a lot on his mind and needed a way to release conflicting emotions.

"I grew up an army brat," Stiletto said, "following my father from one point to another. It was only natural I joined too. Regular infantry at first, then Special Forces.

Got married somewhere in the middle. We had a daughter named Felicia."

"Your wife's name?"

"You can check the file."

Gargarin nodded. He made a note.

Stiletto frowned but checked a smart reply. He imagined the note. *Patient refused to say wife's name.* It was a significant statement, silent or not. Scott cleared his throat. He started talking to keep from thinking. "I was going to retire, start a security consulting job, but my wife died."

Patient refused to say wife's name...

"What happened?"

"Cancer."

...because he's never truly dealt with her loss.

"Uh-huh."

Keep talking and he won't force you to admit it.

"About the same time, well...after the funeral, my daughter stopped talking to me. I don't know why."

"You two don't communicate at all?"

"I call on Christmas and her birthday. A few times in between. I don't know why she shuts me out. Maybe because I was always gone and she didn't feel like she knew me. I don't know. I've gone in circles trying to figure out what I did."

Gargarin nodded and made another note. "And?"

"I was at loose ends. No wife, no daughter, no prospects. I told the security job I wouldn't be available when my wife got sick. But later, I talked to a friend who helped me get into the CIA."

"But you aren't at CIA any longer, correct?"

"Right. Spent a few years with Ground Branch. Special Activities. All that stuff. I got fired for going on a rogue mission."

"Do anything illegal?"

"In Russia, yes. In the USA, no. A friend of mine in Moscow was in trouble. He was an ally of ours who'd passed good information to us. When my boss said no to helping him, I went anyway."

"I understand. How did you adjust after getting fired?"

Stiletto took a breath. "It was like losing my wife and kid all over again." He was surprised his voice didn't shake, but his right hand trembled. The memories of his forced departure remained painful. "I'd lost another family, and it was my fault for sure, this time. But I had to help my friend. Despite my orders. Does that make sense?"

"Does it make sense to you?"

"On the surface, yes. I had so few friends growing up because we moved all the time, I guess I wanted to take care of the ones I did have." Stiletto pressed his lips together. "But, dammit, the cost was high. Almost too high."

"I see."

"Something the matter?" Stiletto said.

"You're the one talking."

"I don't follow, Doctor."

"I asked for information about you, and you delivered. Now I want to know something else. Can you guess?"

Stiletto swallowed. He cleared his throat. He fidgeted. He knew what the doctor wanted. He wanted to know what Scott hadn't articulated in his background sketch. The doctor wanted to know how it all made him *feel*.

"I answered your question," Stiletto said. "I told you my history. Why does the other part matter?"

"It's why you're here, Scott."

"But—"

"I can ask, but it's better if you tell me."

"Why?"

"Because you need to get the words out."

"Will anything change?" Stiletto said.

"I don't know."

Stiletto grimaced. He didn't see a way out. Like being trapped under fire, the only option was to die fighting. To anybody else, fighting might mean refusing to give Gargarin what he wanted. But the therapist had a point. Stiletto would fight his reluctance to tell the truth. Instead, he would fight to verbalize what he felt, deep down.

He said, "All of that, my family, the CIA, made me very angry."

"Take the CIA out of it."

"Very angry," Stiletto said again. His heart rate increased. "I wasn't ready to lose my wife. And, dammit, Doctor, I don't know where my daughter might be." He raised his voice. "I don't know if she needs anything. Does she need money? I don't even know if she's alive!"

The outburst startled Scott. He waited to catch his breath. He felt like he'd been running. *You have been running. From everything.*

Gargarin made another note.

"What do you think, Scott?"

"I think this is the first time I've admitted how I feel. It all happened so fast I never stopped…"

"And?"

"Can we revisit this later?"

"It's safe to say your daughter is all right."

"How?"

"Has her phone been cut off? No. She's there, she

simply isn't answering you. She hasn't changed the number either."

"Means something, right?"

"Sure. And as long as the cell bill stays paid, we can assume Felicia is doing well enough. You don't have to worry about her finances."

"Fathers worry," Scott said.

"I know. I have three myself."

"Okay."

"Let's go back to the CIA. You get fired. What did you do after?"

"I worked freelance for a bit and then joined The Trust."

"I see."

"My old boss from CIA got canned too and he's at The Trust with me. It's like the old days again. Almost."

"Is that a good thing?"

Stiletto paused a moment. "I think so."

"Why do you hesitate?"

"It's not the same."

"The only constant in life is change," Gargarin said. "Even if we had remained at CIA, General Fleming would have retired eventually. He will still, someday."

"I guess."

"How much action have you seen in the last six months?"

"We stay busy," Stiletto said. "I wrapped a job this morning, actually. It's been hectic, Doctor. One job after another."

"It sounds like you've been through a lot, haven't you? And I don't mean the last six months."

Now Stiletto's voice broke. "Too much." He held his breath, let it out slowly, and tried not to turn into a blubbering mess.

"Why do you do this, Scott?"

The question snapped Stiletto from the verge of tears. His mind focused.

"My father always said, there are the oppressed, and the people who can free them. I took it to heart. When I saw oppression up close, I had to do something. Not out of a sense of revenge for anything done to *me*, but because I had the ability. I could help people. Fight the battles they couldn't. Am I making sense?"

"It doesn't have to make sense to me, Scott. Does it make sense to you?"

"If it's what cost me my family, no. Nothing makes sense right now. It's why I'm talking to you."

"What do you hope to get out of your sessions with me?" the doctor said.

"I want to figure stuff out. Discover what I did wrong."

"What if you didn't do anything wrong?"

"Then I want to stop blaming myself for what's happened."

"Uh-huh."

Gargarin watched him. He didn't make any marks in his notebook. Stiletto wished he would if only to break their eye contact.

"Why do you think it was your fault?"

"Are we getting specific or staying general?"

"You weren't specific. To me, you think everything you've experienced is because of something you did. Are you referring to a single event, or a series of choice over time?"

"I don't—"

"Scott, I want you to focus on what you blame yourself for."

"We'll be here all day."

"You have fifteen minutes left."

Stiletto laughed. It broke the tension for a moment. But only a moment. His face appeared grim again as he considered the doctor's request.

"I can't name one thing. I blame myself for my daughter taking off, for ruining a good career, for fighting battles that never end. And I'm tired, Doctor. Just plain tired."

"You missed something."

"What?"

"Your wife."

"What about her?" Scott said.

"The cancer wasn't your fault."

"How could it be?"

The doctor waited.

"Okay," Stiletto said. "I blame myself for always being gone, or home only a short time, when my wife was alive. We saw each other most when she was sick."

"That's tough."

"You think?"

"What might you have done differently?"

"Not join the army."

"It would have to have been that drastic, wouldn't it? Totally different life choice from the beginning."

Stiletto nodded.

"How does it feel to articulate your answer?"

"I don't know. Numb."

"Fair enough. I'd like you to think about your answer for the rest of the week. When we meet again, let's see if you have a different word for your reaction."

"Work might intrude."

"Get some time off."

"Jesus, Doctor…"

"Is there a problem?"

"Without work, I wouldn't know what to do with myself."

———

Stiletto sat in his car in the parking lot of the medical plaza. His hands shook and he couldn't control his breathing. He'd let out too much at once. He needed time to settle before driving away.

His phone rang. He answered.

"Yes?" His voice shook.

"Scott?"

"Here, sir."

"Are you all right? You sound—"

"I know how I sound, General. What's the problem?"

"I need you back at HQ. We have a crisis in Colombia."

"Thank God," Stiletto said. "I'm on my way."

"Scott?"

"Yes?"

"Take it slow."

"I...Yes, sir. I understand."

Scott hung up. He put the phone away. *Take it slow.* General Ike didn't mean the speed limit. He stopped shaking as he turned his mind to the new mission. The engine fired to life at the press of the starter. Stiletto shoved the gear stick into first and drove away.

CHAPTER FIVE

Somewhere in Colombia

Stiletto had done nothing but sweat for the last three days and nights.

The heat and thick humidity made life in camouflage fatigues hell. Beneath the uniform his skin was covered with annoying wetness.

He lay on his belly with damp earth under him. The unforgiving jungle, full of insects preying on the exposed parts of his skin, surrounded him. Combat gloves covered his hands. Black and green cosmetics covered his face.

Scott and his Trust special action unit had arrived in Colombia seventy-two hours earlier. The mission: rescue a captured fellow agent. Fleming wanted Scott on the job because he knew the captured agent. She had become a close friend. Beth Carrington.

Fleming didn't go into a lot of detail during their meeting.

"Beth has been in Colombia lining up a major project I can't explain now. Some cartel thugs have grabbed her, and we need to get her out. I want you there because she'll need a friendly face, and you might need to take over the project. I'll fill you in on the rest later. Right now, our priority is her."

Stiletto had no argument. He appreciated the mission after his ordeal with Dr. Gargarin.

Stiletto held a SIG-Sauer SG-552 Commando in both hands, the full-auto carbine chambered with the 5.56x45mm NATO cartridge. Derived from the US .223, the 5.56x45 NATO packed more punch. His Colt .45 rode in a holster on his right hip. Other necessary tools adorned his combat webbing.

He was in war mode. Beth was in danger. She'd been held captive too long already, but a clean extraction required planning. Stiletto and his team, along with Beth, wouldn't survive a rushed mission. Even with a life at stake, Scott had to follow procedures. It was the only way to do the job right.

But while they prepped, Beth was running out of time, her condition unknown. No cartel gave captured spies or law enforcement any quarter.

Stiletto's hiding spot overlooked a camp. Intel said Beth was in a warehouse on the far side. Stiletto's job was to find her while the rest of the strike force took care of the cartel troopers. A satchel of high explosive time bombs rode on his back, and he tried not to think he carried enough explosive power to put him on the moon. He'd get Beth out, and blow up the warehouse. Intel also said it was inside the building where the cartel stored heavy weapons.

The Motorola com unit in his right ear had remained

quiet for over an hour. The only way to pass the time was to study the target.

Cartel forces had cleared the wooded area. Smaller buildings were in place for housing. The warehouse on the opposite end of the compound had a creek running behind it. They used the creek as part of their rear security. The water was deep and full of who-knew-what. Approaching from the warehouse side had been an idea Stiletto vetoed.

The com unit clicked. Stiletto listened. The voice of Mike Majors, who'd been in-country with Beth, whispered, "We have a problem."

Majors was a Trust operative Stiletto hadn't met before, but was beginning to like. He was in charge of the mission.

"What is it?" Stiletto asked.

"We are counting twice as many troops as we were told they'd have."

Stiletto waited while Majors paused.

Then: "I think we should abort."

Scott keyed the microphone. "Beth doesn't have the time."

Others in the group chimed in to agree with Stiletto.

"We brought a superior force," Stiletto continued. "We can handle this."

"We might be outnumbered."

"Shoot fast and move faster. I'm not leaving Beth here another night. I'll take my chances alone if I have to."

"Wait one."

Stiletto watched the compound in the ensuing silence. He didn't have the same view as Majors. Stiletto had to take his word as gospel. If they all were killed in the rescue attempt, Beth's situation wouldn't improve. Was Majors right or was it worth the risk?

Dammit!

Scott and Beth Carrington had not seen eye-to-eye on anything the first time they worked together. She was from an old-money New England family, graduate of a proper school and connections via family to the DC political elite. Stiletto was a rough-neck army brat who'd never set foot on a college campus. By the end of their mission, the differences melted away, replaced by mutual respect that grew to friendship.

He didn't have a problem with Majors exercising caution, but they'd done their due diligence, and now was the time to strike. Before Beth ran out of time for good.

Stiletto didn't want to tell her family they'd lost a daughter.

Majors came back over the com link. "We're a go, stand by."

Stiletto cracked a grin and flicked off the safety on the SG-552, and started a countdown in his head. The cartel troops were about to pay a price, in blood, for their misdeeds.

And if he found Beth dead, Stiletto would bring even more hell to the ones responsible.

————

A mortar strike and salvos from a pair of heavy machine guns opened the action.

The mortar impacts shook the ground and explosions rocked the compound. The barracks exploded, each structure spreading fire and flaming debris. The strike force stormed the camp, automatic weapons blazing. The heavy machine gunners, along with snipers, kept the suppressive fire humming.

Stiletto bolted from his hiding spot. His boots pounded the soft ground as he ran forward with the SG-552 tucked into his shoulder. Movement right to left. He pivoted to trigger a burst at a running cartel gunman, the burst catching the trooper mid-stride. The gunman tumbled, fell end-over-end, coming to a stop and no longer moving. A bullet split the air near Stiletto's head as he shifted and triggered shots in a left-to-right pattern. He blasted a pair of gunners leap-frogging their way to him. One fell with a burst of lead through the chest, the other continuing the charge, firing again. Stiletto dove onto his belly, a bullet parking his hair, his follow-up shot from the SIG carbine splitting open the man's belly and turning him and his last meal into a grisly pile in the dirt.

The ground churned around Stiletto, bullets from above. He looked up, left, right—guard tower! The last one standing, somehow missed by the mortar shelling. Stiletto raised his SG-552 and fired. Too high. He adjusted his aim and fired again. The wooden slats forming a barrier in front of the trooper splintered. Too low. The gunner returned fire and missed. Stiletto fired another salvo and emptied the magazine. But he scored. The rounds punched through the gunner's chest and forced him over the barrier behind him. He fell from the tower like a rock.

Stiletto reloaded on the run, slapping in the fresh magazine and zig-zagging for the warehouse thirty yards ahead. The battle raged, the gunfire loud and unceasing, the occasional shout breaking through the cacophony. Cartel shooters fired at him from cover. Stiletto fired back, hitting the ground to roll behind a stack of wooden pallets, more shots chipping at the wood as he burrowed close to the ground. He inched around the side. One burst. Miss. Another. Hit. Gunner down. More rounds hammered the pallets, wood slivers striking his fatigues. One sharp piece of debris felt as if it sliced through his exposed neck.

Stiletto plucked a grenade from his chest rig, pulled the pin, and tossed it around the side. The blast sent a plume of black smoke and orange fire in the sky, lighting up the area briefly, before the black of night took over again. Stiletto popped his head and SG-552 around the side. No more threats. He left the pallets and continued running, staying close to the buildings now, stopping at each corner to scan for hostiles.

Stiletto pounded up the steps of the warehouse entrance, crashing through the door, rolling onto the ground to come up on a knee again. He scanned the area with the muzzle of the SG-552. Nothing but crates greeted him, most still sealed, a few open, with protective straw cushioning visible automatic rifles.

A young man with a narrow face stuck a pistol around one of the crates and fired. The shot flew wide. Stiletto blasted the kid in the face, putting two more rounds into the fallen body as he ran by. Stiletto moved fast up and down the aisles, looking at rifles, grenades, heavy machine guns, and other small arms. Everything the cartel forces needed to continue their reign of terror.

Stiletto keyed his com link. "I'm in the warehouse."

"Where's Beth?" Majors said.

"No sign yet."

"Copy. Resistance is hot but almost contained."

The fighting continued; the crackles of automatic weapons muffled now that he was inside. Stiletto started moving again. He had to find Beth.

Then he heard her cry out.

CHAPTER SIX

She uttered a muffled cry, but the sound cut through the fog of battle enough for Scott to quicken his pace.

He found Beth chained to a wall in a corner, a dirty mattress under her. She sat on the mattress with her legs out, arms above her head and shackled, the steel cuffs digging into her wrists. Ugly purple welts covered her bare arms and face. Her clothes were torn and soiled. She recognized him, eyes pleading for help as he approached.

She choked out, "Scott!"

"Hang on."

He examined the shackles. He needed a key.

"Who has the key, Beth?"

Her eyes closed halfway. Her head dipped.

"Beth! Who has the key?"

"The kid. You shot. Him."

Stiletto ran back to the young gunner he'd killed on entry, searched his pockets, and found the key. He ignored the blood smeared on his hands in the process. Running back to Beth, he freed her wrists. With a gasp of relief, she brought her arms to her body and curled up on the dirty mattress.

"Beth, we gotta go."

She let out a sound Stiletto couldn't comprehend.

"I'll be right back," he told her.

He set his weapon down long enough to get the satchel of explosives off his back. Slinging the carbine and carrying the satchel, he placed the charges at each aisle, setting the timers for three minutes. With the weight off his back, he moved fast, like an Olympic sprinter, gathering Beth and putting her across his shoulders as a final act.

As he bounded out of the warehouse and back into the compound, he shouted over the com that he had Beth and the bombs would go off in three...two...

The warehouse explosion sucked the air out of the compound and Stiletto felt his feet leave the ground a moment. He touched down again but didn't fall. The last thing Beth needed was another injury. Her weight on his back was a tough burden to carry. He didn't want to be responsible for hurting her further.

Debris fell like rain, some pieces on fire, more of the jungle ablaze now. Stiletto rejoined Majors and the strike force. The group was withdrawing the way they'd arrived. The dark jungle remained unforgiving as they plowed through the thick foliage, shouting at each other to keep everyone on track. Stiletto jogged behind Majors, grunting under the strain of carrying Beth, who made no noise. Presently they reached the spot where their vehicles waited. Land Rovers, Land Cruisers, and Hummers, all with engines running. The strike force climbed aboard the vehicles and, appropriately spaced out, made for the main highway.

In the back of a Rover, Beth stretched across the

bench seat running the length of the truck, Stiletto checked her pulse and breathing. A young medic began treating the visible wounds.

"Is she alive?" Majors called from the front seat.

"She's messed up bad, Mike," Stiletto reported.

"Let's get her home."

Stiletto sat and watched Beth's chest rise and fall as the Rover continued on.

———

Carlos Guardado didn't want to leave the confines of the armored Mercedes SUV. He had no choice, though. Leaders had to lead during a crisis.

Twenty-four hours after the raid on the compound and rescue of the American woman, his Mercedes and two large Suburbans drove into the compound. He exited before his gun crew. The gunmen hurried out of the two Suburbans and fanned out around him. Their weapons were ready; they scanned for threats.

Carlos examined the still-smoldering remains of the camp. "This is madness," he said. He started walking. His protective crew moved with him. He looked at the wreckage of the warehouse. It was now only a twisted hulk of charred metal. All the weapons gone. He greeted the remaining camp troops who were still able to walk. The dead and wounded had long been taken away.

Carlos listened to their stories of the attack without comment, but promised they'd receive a bonus for their valiant defense.

He continued the tour. His bodyguard and confidant, Paco Rodrigo, joined him at the edge where the compound met the creek.

The flowing stream suggested peace where there was none.

Paco looked behind them as Carlos watched the water. The bodyguard muttered a string of curses.

"We must find more Americans," Paco said.

"Good luck."

"This is the fourth attack in two months. The American woman told us nothing."

Paco Rodrigo wore a perpetual frown on his rough face. He stood taller than Carlos, but the shorter cartel boss wasn't bothered by Paco's extra inches. He had all the power. Paco existed only to follow orders.

"The time is coming, Carlos, where we must make a statement in return."

"I'm aware. But we must choose carefully. Make them hurt the way they've hurt us."

"You are taking too long."

Carlos looked at Paco with a raised eyebrow.

"Forgive me, Carlos, but—"

"I know you have lost friends. So have I. We can lose money. People, though; people are another matter." He checked his Rolex.

"Why do you keep looking at your watch?" Paco said. "You've been checking it—"

Carlos held up a hand. Paco stopped talking.

"Time is always short, Paco."

"But—"

"No more. It is my business."

The bodyguard grunted and held back a reply.

Carlos turned from the creek and set his eyes on the wreckage once again. But his mind was elsewhere.

They should be in position by now.

Carlos faced Paco. The cartel boss's smooth face remained impassive, but Carlos knew one thing above all else as he studied his old friend. He knew he'd never see Paco again after today.

"We've been here long enough," Carlos said.

With a whistle, Paco Rodrigo ordered the gun crew back into the big Suburbans. He held the Mercedes door open for Carlos and the cartel boss climbed inside.

———

The Mercedes and two Suburbans sped along a winding two-lane road. To the left, the jungle. On the right, the granite wall of a mountain. Destination: Bogota.

Carlos checked his Rolex again.

Any moment now.

He tugged on the cuff of his shirt to cover the gleaming watch. He felt Paco's eyes on him but didn't turn his head. Paco suspected something. Carlos had lived with paranoia long enough to know the signs. But Paco didn't know what he didn't know, which made him dangerous. Were he living another day, he'd look and poke around until he found evidence Carlos was hiding something. He wasn't going to live another day, so Carlos dismissed the concern.

Carlos faced forward and watched the road through the windshield. He began to sweat despite the coolness inside the vehicle. The driver steered the Mercedes around a curve and the road straightened again. No need to check the Rolex now. It was about to happen.

Carlos braced.

Three rapid blasts erupted from the left side of the road, the jungle breathing fire. Thousands of lead projectiles from Claymore mines ripped into the convoy.

The two Suburbans took the worst of the blasts, tipping over with shredded tires, metal twisting; the

SUVs left a trail of sparks as they slammed into the granite slab on the right side. Metal and glass crunched on impact. Men screamed.

Carlos screamed, too, louder than he thought he would, but the violence of the fiery explosions surprised him. The orange sheet of flame assaulted his side of the SUV and the projectile impacts made him doubt the armored capabilities of his favorite vehicle. But only for a second. The plating held and the glass didn't shatter. The driver, in his own panic, lost control. The Mercedes crashed into the rock side as well. The jolting impact threw Carlos and Paco together. Paco seized the opportunity. He pressed Carlos to the floor, covering him with his body, and at the same time drew his autoloading pistol.

From the jungle, men with automatic rifles emerged. They wore green camo uniforms, face paint concealing their features, and moved with speed. Their weapons popped as they opened fire on the Suburbans and cut down the gunners struggling to get out.

Carlos breathed heavily under Paco's weight. *This is it!* Paco yelled for the driver to get moving again, but the driver said he could not. The front wheel was smashed and the steering wheel was jammed.

Rounds smacked against the armored body and bulletproof glass. Paco watched the green-faced attackers spread out, their weapons aimed at the Mercedes. He grinned. What could they possibly achieve against an armored machine such as the one he and Carlos occupied? Then two men stepped from the jungle again with heavy equipment. It only took a moment for Paco to identify what they carried. Shoulder-fired rocket launchers!

The driver screamed as one of the men stopped in

front of the Mercedes and the second faced Carlos's side. Paco snapped his eyes forward. The trooper lifted the shoulder-launcher to bear and aimed at the windshield. The driver cried out a second time. Paco told him to shut up.

"What's happening, Paco?" Carlos said.

"Quiet, *jefe*."

A look out the side chilled Paco's body as the second trooper aimed the rocket launcher directly at his face.

It was now a no-win situation. Paco swallowed the lump in his throat. The SUV's armor was no match for anti-tank weapons such as the rockets. Paco didn't want to die, but he also didn't want to be arrested.

"Paco."

"Not now, *jefe*."

"Paco, listen to me."

A trooper on the side of the road shouted, "Exit the vehicle or get roasted, your choice."

Sweat dropped into Paco's eyes. He wiped with the back of his hand. He felt more sweat on the palm of his right hand, but didn't want to let go of his gun. He'd never felt so useless. He had no way to fulfill his duty. The sinking feeling in his gut suggested surrender was the only way out.

"Ten seconds!"

Carlos snapped, "Let me out!"

"No, *jefe*."

"There's no other way!"

Paco cursed in disgust. He shifted to allow Carlos to rise.

"At least we will live," Carlos said. He slid across the seat, opened the door, and stepped out onto the hot pavement. He raised his hands.

"I am Carlos Guardado! I am the man you want. There is no need for further bloodshed."

Carlos motioned for Paco and his driver to step out. Paco exited first. He still held his pistol.

Carlos glanced at the wrecked Suburbans. He felt a twinge of guilt. His eight-man crew lay on the pavement. Not one moved. The blood on the asphalt told Carlos all he needed to know. They had been good men. Very loyal. But there could be no witnesses.

None.

The green-face who had spoken stepped forward. "Surrender the pistol."

"Paco, please," Carlos said. He reached for his bodyguard's gun. Paco glared at him. Carlos tugged. Paco let go over the gun.

Carlos gripped the warm pistol.

"I'm sorry, my loyal friend," Carlos said. He raised the gun.

Paco's smile vanished as he looked into the barrel of his own weapon. His face became a mask of confusion and then shock. Carlos shot Paco in the head. The crack of the pistol echoed along the road. Before Paco's body hit the ground, Carlos shifted to the cowering driver. Another shot. The driver fell dead.

Carlos faced the green-face leader and held out the gun.

"I'm all yours," the cartel leader said.

The green-face took the pistol. "Follow us, Mr. Guardado. We have transport waiting."

The green-faced men hustled Carlos into the jungle. They ran hard, keeping Carlos in the center of their group. Carlos huffed to keep up. He might have had a slender build, but he wasn't in shape for a run in boots not made for such activity and doing so on overgrown terrain. But he kept the pace. He had to. The extraction was good. Now he had the rest of his life to live for. Once his family joined him, all would be right with the world.

Everything had gone according to plan.

woman, but he was displeased. He held the earpiece and was quiet. Now he had the recorded call. He now knew...

arm of his small-clothed hand. If would help later when he...

pretty.

Everyone could you...

CHAPTER SEVEN

Stiletto paced his hotel room. Bogota was nice but he couldn't see any of the sights or enjoy the culture. He'd left the drapes closed, but sunlight crept in around the edges of the drapes. There was a building across the street, and a sniper on the roof had an easy shot at his window. He wasn't taking the chance. The lamps provided the light in the room. He looked at the desk against the wall where his laptop sat. General Ike's promised call was ten minutes late.

He wanted to know more about why Fleming insisted he *stay* in Bogota after recovering Beth. He understood the need to replace her, but what her assignment had been, he had no idea. Mike Majors had not provided any information either. He'd told Scott it was best to let Fleming fill in the blanks.

There also wasn't any news on Beth, which bothered him. After a day, he'd expected news. Good or bad. Maybe no news was the best news. She'd been alive when they transferred her to a medical jet home. The strike force medic had managed to get her stable and hooked to an IV. Dehydration was her biggest problem; the injuries weren't as bad as they might have been, but they were bad. She hadn't been raped. She'd regained consciousness long enough to tell them so, and also tell Majors who was responsible for her capture. Majors held back the information from Scott, who figured he'd ask Fleming first thing. He wanted answers. If he was going to complete the assignment, he had to know enough to do the job.

He decided to stop pacing and watch television to fill the time. If Fleming was late, he had a reason.

Stiletto turned on a news report and immediately wished he had left the wide-screen blank and silent. He watched a report on a series of random police killings. Investigators believed the killers were working independently of the cartels, but the murders were certainly in retaliation for recent police and government raids. Witnesses reported two killers in a truck and the shooter preferred a shotgun. They reportedly tracked their quarry, waited for an opportunity, and fired from the vehicle when they had a clear shot. Six dead cops, so far.

Stiletto pressed his lips together and shook his head. Yet another example of senseless violence. It would only stop with a violent response from good guys with their own guns. Such an attitude might upset the peaceniks and make the philosophers scratch their heads, but Stiletto wasn't in the business of talking. He was in the business of killing men who thought murder was a tool of their trade, who saw no shame in ripping a loved one from somebody's life, all in the name of what? Drugs? Profit? It made no sense. And the only kind of response human garbage such as the cop killers deserved was a bullet. The peaceniks could wave their signs and wear their pussy hats and complain all day, but in the end, they were nothing but a bunch of naïve children who probably still believed in Santa Claus.

Stiletto turned off the TV in disgust. He took a deep breath and put the frustration aside. Being mad wasn't productive. He looked at the laptop again. Where the hell was General Ike?

The computer beeped. Finally! Stiletto moved to the table and sat. The General appeared on-screen.

"Sorry I'm late," Fleming said. "How's the weather?"

"Never mind. How's Beth?"

"She's doing well, Scott. Last check she was sleeping. Doctors have her sedated right now, and they're watching her."

"Okay. The weather here is hot and wet. I'm sure there's a dirty joke in there somewhere."

"I'll try and find it. We could use a good joke right now."

"What's ruined your sense of humor, sir?"

"The Hardison situation," General Ike said. "He's the reason I was late."

"Is he giving you trouble?"

"No. In fact, he's cooperating and providing decent info. We told him to talk or we'd turn him over to the CIA. He wants to save his neck. But the CIA is giving us trouble. They are *pissed*. They want the man and the device. We've told them to kick rocks for now, but they may escalate."

"How?"

"This wasn't exactly *legal*, Scott. They can make a lot of trouble if they want to waste the time. We may need to call in a few favors if they turn up the heat."

"They'll back down," Stiletto said. "They're humiliated. And probably deserve it. Hardison hacked our satellite tracking, and they didn't detect him. They also failed to bid high enough for the device, and didn't grab him. We've upstaged their whole operation. They'll cool off."

"It's not your problem any longer, Scott. I'm sure you have questions about Bogota instead."

"What the heck am I doing here, yes, sir, please explain."

"We have a sensitive project to finish, one started before you and I joined The Trust. All we have to go on is the file my predecessor left behind. Unfortunately, he is not alive to tell us more. But I need you to take Beth's place and complete the mission."

"Okay."

"The nature of this project will make you think we've gone to the zoo."

Stiletto sighed. "Let's hear it."

"We need to bring an informant and her daughter out of Bogota. They're part of the Guardado cartel."

"The people who grabbed Beth?"

"Exactly."

"Who are the informants?"

"The husband and wife in charge of the cartel."

"I think there's a problem with our connection, sir."

"No, you heard me correctly. The leaders of the Guardado Cartel, Carlos and Jackeline, have been feeding us information for the last five years. They've reduced not only the effectiveness of their own organization, but their rivals as well."

"I don't believe it," Stiletto said.

"The husband, Carlos, came to us about exchanging information for safe harbor in the US."

"Nuts."

"It was the wife's idea." The General consulted notes. "They made the decision because of their daughter, who was ten years old at the time. My predecessor made a different deal. We kept them in business while they provided intel on themselves and the competition. Their knowledge helped us make a huge dent in the drug traffic out of Colombia."

"Could have fooled me," Stiletto said.

"I know, I know. But it would have been much worse had we not had their data."

"Why are we bringing them in now?"

"The daughter is fifteen. They've demanded we honor the agreement. I spoke with Number One and he decided it's time."

Stiletto respected the man referred to as "Number One." He was the top cog in The Trust. Edward Northwood was one of the three men who formed the organization. Scott had yet to meet the other two.

"I'm not exactly on board with this, sir," Stiletto said. "Not after what happened to my niece."

"Understandable. Making deals with cartel bosses isn't popular with anybody. Even *I'd* rather pass."

"Explain to me how the Guardados captured Beth."

"There is a man in the cartel we need to remove. His name is Manny Valdes. He's the one who ordered Beth's capture, and the only reason we knew where to find her was because of Carlos and Jackeline."

"So you're saying this Valdes person saw Beth hanging around, got suspicious, and grabbed her?"

"Correct."

"Uh-huh."

"I figured you'd understand getting the daughter out, right?"

Stiletto didn't reply, but the General hit a nerve, and had done so to manipulate Stiletto's decision-making. They might have been close, but Fleming was still a spy master. You said whatever was necessary to get your people to do what you wanted.

It was one thing to refuse to help two adults who, despite "finding religion" or whatever caused their change of heart, had flooded the world with poison. But the kid couldn't be blamed. If the Guardados were taking a risk to save their child, and feeding info to the US for five years, their efforts qualified as a major risk; if their subversion was ever discovered, they'd be gutted and hung from a bridge. Their kid too. Maybe they were the kind of people he *should* be helping.

"Tell me more," Stiletto said, "about the information they've given us. What good has it done?"

Fleming consulted his notes again. "Intel on their competition, as I said. Because of them we closed down smuggling routes, drug tunnels; took out a few major players. All because Carlos and Jackeline are serious. Your skepticism is normal, but I have to say, from the evidence, it appears they worked in good faith."

"So all three?"

"Only the mother and daughter. We recovered Carlos a few hours ago. He's on his way here."

"You didn't do all three at once?"

"We have to keep up appearances. And the Manny Valdes fellow I mentioned. He needs to be taken out before we get Jackeline and her daughter."

"He angling for a takeover or something?"

"He's a close friend of the family, and they don't want him to find out what they've done."

"And come after them later."

"Yes."

Stiletto pressed his lips together. He didn't want the job. He didn't believe the story. Cartel people weren't real people—they were snakes in human skin. It wasn't against the law, anywhere, to kill them. They were no better than cockroaches. There had to be another agenda somewhere, and without the people who made the original deal, Stiletto felt like they were operating in the dark.

But he was already in Bogota.

And he couldn't refuse General Ike. If the boss thought they were on the level, he had to *try*. Give them the benefit of the doubt. And be ready to kill them at the slightest hint of treachery.

"All right, General, I'm here. I'll do it."

"I know it isn't easy for you to say so."

"Uh-huh."

"Coordinate with Mike Majors from here."

"Keep me updated on Beth, please."

"Will do."

Stiletto ended the video call and folded his hands in front of his face. Of all the lousy assignments…

But this was the spy business. Sometimes you had to use bad guys to catch bigger bad guys. He didn't have to like it. He only had to follow orders.

CHAPTER EIGHT

Dust hung in the air but Jackeline Guardado paid no attention.

She leaned against a wooden fence watching her daughter Sofia. The teenager rode a horse back and forth through a line of barrels. The animal's hoofs churned the dirt and sent a thick dust cloud overhead.

It was a moment of tranquility following the stressful hours following news of Carlos's "capture" reaching the hacienda.

Sofia urged her horse faster as she zig-zagged through the barrels. She reached the end of the line, flung her horse into a U-turn, and started the course again.

Jackeline watched her daughter with relief when she saw the joy on the 15-year-old's face. Jackeline had insisted they leave the house and run her horse to get their minds off the bad news. For her, of course, it wasn't bad news, but the first stage of a plan. But Sofia didn't know the plan, and thought her father's disappearance was real.

Jackeline turned away a moment to look at the open country. A ton of acreage surrounded their hacienda, itself not small at all. Green mountains in the distance, fields of tall grass, sky above clear and blue and majestic. She hated to have to leave it behind, but life was full of times of sacrifice. She and Carlos would find another paradise once they reunited.

Jackeline turned her attention back to her daughter. She marveled at how beautiful she was becoming. Sofia was a spitting image of her mother at fifteen, same long black hair, dark eyes; but thinner, and she had her father's bony chin.

Sofia U-turned the horse again and leaned forward in the saddle for her next run. The girl's ponytail bounced like the horse's tail as the animal darted through the gaps. Another cloud of dust drifted by.

Somebody coughed behind her.

Jackeline wasn't startled or worried. She had enough armed gunners within shouting distance to neutralize any threat, especially in the current heightened state of alert. Jackeline turned to smile at the woman approaching.

"Can we talk away from this dust, Jackie?"

Amaya Olmos was Jackeline's personal adviser and bodyguard. Carlos had Paco, she had Amaya. But Amaya was also her best friend and an aunt to Sofia. Amaya's toned and athletic build contrasted with Jackeline's voluptuous physique.

Jackeline left the fence. They moved to a cluster of nearby trees. The shade blotted out the bright sun.

"What is it, Amaya?"

"Valdes is coming."

Jackeline stifled a curse. She put her hands on her

hips and her face became a stoic mask. A hard shell. Her poker face.

"Are you okay?" Amaya said.

"Valdes will expect immediate retaliation."

"You've been doing this for five years. Another couple of days—"

"Will be the worst of all."

"Think of Sofia."

"All I *do* is think of Sofia." The mask cracked. Jackeline's eyes widened and her neck flushed red, but she kept her voice low. "What if the Americans betray us? They have Carlos. They can easily leave us hanging."

"Carlos won't let them. Stop it, Jackie. You're creating fear where there should be none. There is enough real fear to consider."

Jackeline let out a breath. She was paranoid by nature. As a cartel leader, there was always a target on her back. Somebody always had their eye on the big chair.

Amaya said, "You have to see it through. It's the only way."

"I wish there was another."

The wind shifted. Dust drifted their way. Jackeline and Amaya watched Sofia slow her horse and begin a circle of the pen to cool the animal down.

"You are a good friend, Amaya."

"The three of you are the only family I have."

A male voice called out, "Mrs. Guardado!"

"Here comes Valdes," Amaya said.

Jackeline moved her back to the trees. Amaya positioned herself ahead and to the left so when Manny Valdes reached them, she stood between the two. Jackeline Guardado did not trust Manny Valdes. At all. Not one bit. Her husband might have been blinded to

Valdes's true nature by childhood loyalty, but she was not. Valdes had come to them a drug addict in need of drying out. What Jackeline feared was his idea he should have been second-in-command instead of her. And how he might try for a takeover with Carlos gone.

A target on her back. *Always.*

She knew from Carlos that Valdes had made it clear several times Jackeline, a woman, never should have a position of power in the cartel. Carlos had not caved and kept his wife in her spot. Valdes wasn't the only one upset about the move, and Carlos took flak from friends and rivals alike. It simply wasn't done. Cartel wives traditionally remained invisible, in the background, and never in charge of anything other than the kids.

"I should have been there, Mrs. Guardado."

Jackeline let him see a small smile. It was a smile full of the knowledge he wasn't allowed to address her in any other way. She knew the rule boiled his blood.

"Nonsense," she said. "You have your responsibilities. If Paco couldn't protect him, nobody could." *Poor Paco.* "You'd have been killed too." She paused as she realized several potential problems might have been solved had Valdes had his wish. *Too bad.* "All we can do now is our duty," she concluded.

"The American woman gave us nothing," Valdes said. "If we had broken her—"

"We don't know the Americans had anything to do with this, or what your mysterious woman was doing around here," Jackeline said. She had not approved of Beth Carrington's capture. It was an effort started by Valdes and reported after the fact. She and her husband had had no choice but to go along, though Carlos did tell the Americans where their Valdes had taken their captured agent.

Valdes said, "Our informants say nobody has brought Carlos to the usual detention facilities. Right now, it's like he's a ghost. Who else but American agents? They *would* take him somewhere we can't find."

Valdes stepped closer but Amaya blocked him with an arm. He moved back.

"But we will find him," Valdes continued. "They will not keep Carlos from us."

Jackeline nodded. She turned to watch Sofia jump from the horse, open the gate in the fence, and lead the horse toward the stables.

Watching Sofia covered the hesitation she felt regarding her continued "performance." But she had to continue. Valdes could not sense any weakness. To remain quiet when faced with an *expected* course of action, despite being an upset wife, would only arouse his suspicions.

"Until we know where my husband is, I want action. I want our best shooters on the street. I want examples made of any US drug agent they find. If they aren't responsible, we'll kill them until they tell us who to see." She turned hot eyes on Valdes and saw him blanch. "Understand?"

"It will be done."

Manny Valdes excused himself and started back to the house. The white multi-story building reflected the warm sun.

Amaya said, "Jackie—"

"*What?*"

"Targeting American agents—"

"I know it's a risk but what else can I do? I will get word to them. In the meantime, they will have to shoot faster than our people."

"And if he doesn't give the order? What if Valdes

begins building support to take over and get rid of you, me, and Sofia?"

"Ask your, um...*suitor* to tell you if he tries anything."

"I can ask."

"*Encourage* him, Amaya. We are talking life and death."

"Of course." Amaya's face turned sour. "I regret I have but one vagina to sacrifice for our secret."

Jackeline scoffed. "God, you make me feel horrible. You know I didn't mean to suggest—"

"It's the stress. Let's forget it. Let's get Sofia and see about some food. You look like you need something to eat."

"I think you're right."

The two women left the tree and walked to the stables. They didn't speak, and if Amaya felt the same weight on her shoulders as Jackeline, her friend hid her feelings well. Then again, Amaya had learned to hide things as part of a survival mechanism Jackeline hoped to never need to duplicate.

They found Sofia in the stables brushing her horse.

CHAPTER NINE

The three-story hotel was brightly colored which served as a nice contrast against the clear blue sky and green backdrop of the mountains at the edge of the city.

Manny Valdes drove alone. Normally he'd have a driver named Dante Costa behind the wheel, but his mission had nothing to do with the Guardado Cartel. His errand was personal. If Jackeline discovered what he was doing, she'd feed him to alligators.

He had an obligation to take advantage of Carlos being gone. He intended to take *full* advantage of the gap in leadership. There was no way Jackeline could do what her husband had. Motherhood had made her soft. Without Sofia, Valdes had no doubt Jackeline's former ruthlessness never would have faded. She'd have remained a vivid fixture with her pink AK-47 and the willingness to use it against their enemies.

She might have been a good *sicaria* before Carlos claimed her, but a cartel leader she was not.

To achieve his own goal, Manny Valdes needed to adopt the same level of ruthlessness, but he needed help.

Shortening Jackeline Guardado's lifespan, and those of Amaya Olson and the brat daughter. The meeting was about his plan for accomplishing the objective. It had been in motion for months and demanded the killing of Carlos to start, but Valdes couldn't bring himself to shoot the one man who had always believed in him.

Manny Valdes turned into the hotel parking lot. Only two cars sat in the otherwise empty lot. Two sedans near the entrance. Uniformed chauffeurs stood beside each car. Valdes knew from past meetings they were armed with compact submachine guns under their driving jackets.

The two men Valdes was meeting had bought out the hotel for the day. They could have met anywhere, but the little hotel at the edge of Bogota wasn't likely to be on the radar of Guardado spies.

Valdes stopped the car beside the other two sedans. He gave his face a last glance in the visor mirror. Thick black hair, slicked; mustache, trimmed; dark eyes and sharp jaw. He was well-muscled, and unarmed. He felt confident he could handle a threat without a gun of his own. Guns didn't solve everything, but they sure solved 95% of whatever problems he could think of.

He nodded to the chauffeurs who did not acknowledge him as he crossed to the entrance.

Valdes did not have security of his own, but did not fault his "friends" from being theirs. He had no reason to fear the cartel leaders he was meeting, but he wondered if his lack of an entourage was a sign he had yet to recruit any Guardado shooters to his side. He hoped they didn't ask.

The chilly lobby was a welcome change from outside. Two more bodyguards in dark suits stood outside a conference room off the lobby. Valdes approached them. A quick pat down satisfied the pair he had no weapon.

Valdes entered the conference room. It was small, the carpet a dark brown, the walls white. The table was solid oak. Bright and clean all around. One wall was actually three panes of glass looking in on an office center full of copy machines and computers.

Two men sat at the table. Two well-groomed men who looked mean. Bottles of water sat at the three chairs. Valdes pulled out the empty chair and sat. He regarded the other two faces curiously. Neither smiled. Their dark eyes showed something less than friendliness.

"We are glad you made it, Mr. Valdes," said the man sitting to Valdes's right.

Jorge Ramirez ran the northern branch of Colombia's Beltran-Leyva Cartel. His face looked like a rock with chips and crevices, and his age didn't help. He might have been rugged and handsome in his youth; as gravity exerted itself, he no longer resembled a pinup. Ramirez was simply another old man; albeit one who commanded an army.

"You sound like you weren't sure I'd be here," Valdes said.

"We weren't," said the second man at the table.

Fausto Sanchez glared at Valdes while twisting the cap off his bottle of water. He twisted like he was snapping somebody's neck. He passed the bottle to Valdes.

"You look thirsty."

"I have my own, thanks." Valdes touched his bottle but didn't open it.

Sanchez was the top torpedo with the Plancarte Cartel, which not only had fingers in the northern region with Ramirez's group, but a major presence in southern Colombia too.

"I don't understand," Valdes said. "I thought we were meeting to talk about our progress."

"*Lack* of progress is more accurate," Ramirez said. "We have decided that if you do not deliver results soon, we will cancel the agreement. There is no excuse for more delays after the removal of Carlos Guardado."

"There is no reason to cancel, Jorge."

"Then *why* is the woman still alive? Carlos being taken is the chance you say you've been waiting for, as you apparently lack the will to kill him."

"I have not yet consolidated my position," Valdes said. "Many of the troops are loyal to Carlos still. They *will* be a threat."

"You're soft," Sanchez said. "Never mind the loyal troops. What does that even mean? They are loyal to whoever's in charge. When you're in the chair, they follow *your* orders. If they refuse, somebody who does follow your orders will kill them."

"It is understandable," Ramirez said, "how you cannot bring down the guillotine on a person who saved you from the streets, but he is gone now. The woman deserves no such loyalty."

Valdes didn't reply.

Ramirez continued, "But if we do not see action soon, the deal is off, and we will put *your* head on the chopping block for wasting our time."

Valdes let out a breath. "Are you giving me a time limit?"

"Do you need one?"

"I'm asking."

"We are only telling you to do what you have been promising for months," Ramirez said. "You should not require a deadline. But to humor you, we will give you, what? Five days? Five days will be sufficient."

Ramirez turned to Sanchez for confirmation. Sanchez nodded.

To Valdes, Ramirez said, "Five days. Then your head if you have not delivered."

Valdes said, "All right." He left the chair, and the room, without saying goodbye. He felt grateful to return to his car. He glanced at the chauffeurs as he turned for the exit, but they remained stoically uninterested.

Valdes drove and tried to quiet his anger. Ramirez and Sanchez had no right to make their demands. After all, the alliance had been *his* idea. He'd come to *them* with the idea to form a Super Cartel, a drug trafficking triangle with which to flood the world with narcotics. They'd have more resources than any other cartel. They'd be richer than they already were. And unstoppable.

Ramirez had been correct on one point. It was tough to destroy those who had helped you out of the gutter after alcohol and drugs had turned you into a living dead man. Carlos Guardado had found Valdes in such a condition ten years earlier. They had been friends since grade school, but Valdes had fallen on hard times. His addiction didn't help. Carlos gave him a job with authority, and helped him regain his self-respect. Valdes quit the junk in return. An addict working for a cartel might have been ironic, but Valdes wasn't the only one. He *was* the only sober addict among those in the organization who sampled the cartel's product.

Carlos may have done what he thought was right, but as time went on Valdes saw Carlos fail to steer the ship on the proper course. Raids from the Colombian and United States governments crippled distribution. They lost key people to arrest and assassination. They weren't the only cartel suffering, but to Valdes, it seemed Carlos and Jackeline were the only cartel leaders *not* trying to figure out the cause of the misfortune. They *had* to have a spy on the inside, somebody informing on them, and neither Carlos nor his wife saw any urgency to ferret out the traitor.

Now with Carlos removed by chance or luck, Jackeline had to go.

Super Cartel. Valdes said the words out loud. A Super Cartel with him in charge of one side of the triangle. The fulfillment of a dream.

And he wasn't going to let *the woman* destroy his dream.

Hands tight on the wheel, he made his way back to the Guardado hacienda.

Five days?

He'd do it in three.

CHAPTER TEN

Returning to the hacienda wasn't a quick trip. Valdes found himself stuck in traffic. When his cell phone rang, he was glad for the distraction.

"What?"

"It's Estivo."

"You have information for me?"

"Potential safe house used by American agents."

"Where?"

Estivo gave Valdes the address. The street hustler and cartel spy was one of many alerted to Jackeline's order to find US drug agents.

"How did you locate the house?" Valdes said.

"Neighborhood kids," Estivo replied. "They play football in the street and keep seeing *gringos* going in and out."

"Expect a bonus if this works out, Estivo."

Valdes ended the call and dialed another number. The second conversation was short. He spoke to one of his men at a Guardado front in the city. He gave the other man the location provided by Estivo, description, and an action order. Jackeline would have her "strike back" soon.

Valdes put his phone away and inched through traffic. He returned to the problem of how to remove Jackeline from power and get shooters on his side.

What if he found out *she* was the spy?

The idea took shape in his head. He wouldn't need proof when *rumor* might achieve the same results. The entire cartel wondered how the raids happened, how their secrets seemed anything but...

Valdes grinned.

Traffic wasn't so bad any longer.

———

Stiletto arrived at Mike Majors' hotel room and knocked on the door. Majors answered. He matched Scott in height but had darker hair with a bulkier build.

"Talk to the boss?" Majors said.

"He told me to coordinate with you now."

"Come on in."

Stiletto entered the room. Majors locked the door. The room matched Scott's except the bed and television were in opposite spots.

"Let's gather 'round the laptop," Majors said, "and I'll show you the players."

Stiletto said, "Got any beer?"

"Isn't it early?"

"After my chat with Fleming, I need a drink."

"Check the fridge." Majors tended to the laptop while Stiletto opened the mini-refrigerator in a corner. He grabbed a bottle of local brew. Majors refused his own.

Stiletto popped the cap and stood behind Majors as he worked on the laptop.

"We'll go over the extraction plan when we meet the others at the safe house," Majors said.

"Who's with you?"

"McCoy and Ellis."

"Are the three of you going to be enough?"

"This wasn't meant to be a big operation, Scott."

"Where's the strike team we hit the camp with?"

"They've gone home."

"Great," Stiletto grumbled. He swallowed a mouthful of beer.

"Right now, I want to give you an idea of who you'll be dealing with on the cartel side."

Pictures appeared on the laptop screen. "Meet Carlos and Jackeline Guardado. Certainly, they are no saints but they've turned to the good side." Majors rotated the screen so Stiletto had a better view.

"There's Carlos," Majors said. "Short, clean-cut, conservative clothing choices. Very much a low-key fellow. Inherited the cartel from his father. He ran the operation with an iron fist. He might look small, but he was quite ruthless, and remains so." Majors manually cycled through more pictures of Carlos. Most featured his wife, but Scott focused on the man. He looked so plain and unassuming, he might have been an accountant, engineer, or lawyer in a different life.

"What about the wife?" Stiletto said.

"She has a more flamboyant background. Cooled off after her daughter came along."

"This whole thing hinges on the kid, doesn't it?"

"Correct," Majors said. "If they had not had their daughter, we might be looking at terminating both of these people with prejudice."

"A much more appealing prospect."

"You got a personal beef with these people?"

"People like them. It's a long story. Continue."

Majors changed the pictures to Jackeline Guardado. They showed a curvy and busty woman with long black hair, in most cases too much makeup, and clothes too tight. Stiletto noted she wore them well, but they made her look like she shopped from the kid's rack. She wanted to show off all the curves, and posed in her fancy outfits in front of flashy cars. She looked out of place beside her husband. Another picture showed her firing a pink AK-47 at a shooting range. Stiletto laughed.

"It's for real," Majors said. "Her signature weapon. She's used it in combat."

"When?"

"She was part of a teenaged *sicaria* group. Got out of it when she met her husband. She's reportedly a good shot."

"Uh-huh."

Majors clicked another shot. "This is the photo she took that made her want to change her ways. She's the one who convinced Carlos to defect, if Fleming didn't say so."

"He didn't."

The picture showed a five-year-old girl in a pink jumper laying on a pile of US dollars. The baby displayed a broad smile.

"Kid doesn't seem to mind." Stiletto frowned. "So this is when she didn't want the little girl—"

"Growing up just like her," Majors said. "Jackeline's father was involved in the drug trade too. She's been on the inside in one way or another her entire life."

"I've seen stranger conversions."

"Want a rundown of all the stuff they helped us close down?"

"The General provided those details. What I want to know is how we're getting them out."

"Then let's get to the safe house and we'll go over the plan. McCoy and Ellis are waiting."

Stiletto finished his beer.

———

As Stiletto and Majors began their drive to The Trust's safe house, a seventh police killing occurred. But this time, the killers made a mistake.

Simon Benitez, newly appointed commander of the Bogota police anti-narcotics squad, drove his Chevy SUV along the smooth streets heading home from head-quarters. His wife had lunch waiting for him at their home. Lunch at home was a weekly event for them, but today was the first time in two weeks he'd been able to keep the date. He wasn't a street cop anymore. His days were spent dealing with administrative duties or meetings about ongoing operations. He was happy to let younger men have a shot at the action now.

Benitez had worn a badge most of his adult life. He joined the police force the day after his discharge from the army. The goal was to follow in his father's footsteps. It didn't take long for Benitez to earn the reputation as an honest cop who made good arrests and helped prose-cutors send bad guys to prison. He knew combating the cartels would expose him to a different level of danger, but he felt ready for the challenge.

Stopping for a red light, Benitez drummed the fingers of his left hand on the steering wheel. He noticed a truck inching up on his left side but didn't consider it a threat. But his eyes didn't leave the truck either. When the passenger window rolled down and the snout of a shotgun emerged, Benitez reacted. He clawed for the pistol on his hip only to have the seat belt get in the way of a clean draw. He looked down to move the belt aside.

His world snapped to black.

CHAPTER ELEVEN

The swarthy assassin held the Remington 870 with casual indifference. He liked the American shotgun for its ease of operation, and the fact he'd taken the weapon from the first cop he and the man behind the wheel of the truck had killed.

Bruno Puig, the driver, and Marcos Laguna, the shot-gunner, weren't part of any of the cartels. They were twentysomething roughnecks *trying* to earn their way into the ranks. How better than to kill a bunch of cops?

Bruno eased alongside the Chevy SUV as Benitez the cop waited at the light. Bruno stopped only a few inches from the car in front of him. He looked at Marcos with a raised eyebrow, and the swarthy man nodded. Marcos pumped the Remington's action. Yeah, he could make the shot. Marcos powered down his window, stuck the 870 out and pulled the trigger. He saw Benitez going for his gun but the cop had no chance. At such close range, the pellet blast blew the side window of the SUV clean out of the driver's door frame. The rest of the steel balls passed through to cut open Benitez's neck and shower the cabin with bits of flesh and a spray of red.

Marcos held tight as Bruno spun the wheel, floored the gas, and knocked the car in front of them forward as he executed a sharp U-turn. He cut across the center median, and left a trail of rubber and smoke as he accelerated away.

Neither killer said a word.

But two witnesses saw them. Two men with guns of their own who had no intention of letting the pair in the truck get away.

———

"Holy shit!" Mike Majors shouted. The thunder of the shotgun blast still lingered as the truck launched into a U-turn. Stiletto, beside Majors, turned in his seat to track the truck and look at the pair in front. The killers from the news report; no mistake.

"Get after 'em!" Stiletto shouted. "Go!"

"Read my mind!" Majors replied. Drivers ahead moved forward as the light changed; they wanted to get away from the murder scene. Others stood outside their cars, hurriedly shouting into cell phones. Traffic on the opposite road, having stopped short to avoid colliding with the truck, began to move forward again, but then Mike Majors peeled out. He wrenched the car into a U-turn of its own. A screech of tires and horn blasts sounded behind them as they sped off in pursuit.

"Faster, Mike!" Stiletto hauled his customized Colt from the speed rig under his left arm. He flicked off the safety.

The truck maintained a high speed as Majors stepped

harder on the accelerator. He dodged slower cars to catch up.

"You got a plan?" Majors asked.

"I plan to improvise." Stiletto said.

"Sounds good to me!"

"Get us closer!" Stiletto rolled down his window. Wind rushed into the car.

Majors passed blue and yellow city buses. Trees lined the road, making sudden maneuvers dangerous. Stiletto didn't want them going up on the sidewalk, and not only because they might hit a person; they'd *for sure* hit a tree.

The truck sped through a red light and Majors followed, hand on the horn to keep other drivers from going through. The shotgunner looked back at them through the truck's rear window. Stiletto held up his gun. The shotgunner shifted to his knees to open the sliding back window.

Majors said, "Our insurance doesn't cover shotgun damage!"

"Then we better not get hit!"

Stiletto unsnapped his seat belt and leaned out the window. As the shotgunner poked out the 870, Stiletto fired twice. One .45 hollow-point hit low, under the window glass, and the other smacked into the edge of the truck's roof. The shotgunner didn't retreat, and Majors jerked the wheel, cutting off a car behind them, to avoid his return fire. The roadway cleared a little as drivers pulled over at the first sound of gunfire; people on the street sought cover. Another day in Bogota. They were used to getting out of the way of bullets. But Stiletto knew if he and Majors didn't neutralize the driver and its passengers quickly, they might end up with civilian casualties. Stiletto didn't want *any*.

The truck made a sharp turn onto Av. Calle 26.

Another long stretch of roadway, wider than the previous street, and it ended in the green mountains east of the city. Majors followed. The shotgunner fired again but missed. The truck's driver weaved in and out of lanes and threw off his partner's aim.

"Don't let them get away, Mike!"

"No chance."

The truck powered through another red light, collided with the front end of a sedan. The impact crunched the sedan's front fender and sent the car into a spin. The sedan drifted into the intersection. Majors spun the wheel left, screeched the tires as he avoided the sedan, and steered right to line up on the road again.

Stiletto held on and kept his eyes forward. The truck started up an incline into the mountains. He hoped the occupant of the sedan wasn't hurt.

The mountain road went into a series of sharp twists and turns. Both vehicles slowed a little. Majors whipped the wheel left and right to keep up. Stiletto braced in the window, wind pounding his face. He gripped the Colt .45 tightly. All he needed was one clear shot.

Another sharp right. Majors caught up. A shotgun blast smacked the road in front of the car. Stiletto fired twice. The truck's back wheel exploded. Pieces of shredded rubber bounced away in a shower of sparks as the steel rim bit into the asphalt.

The truck screeched into a pullout on the right shoulder. Majors stopped with a jolt ten yards behind. Stiletto and Majors piled out and squatted behind their car.

The shotgunner jumped out and fired once. As he pumped the action, Stiletto shot him twice in the chest. The shotgunner's face went from concentration to shock, his eyes bulging in surprise. The hollow-point punched out his back, tearing chunks of flesh with them. The shotgunner collapsed near the ruined back rim.

The driver hopped out. He didn't carry a shotgun. The weapon he swung on Stiletto and Majors was s stubby Ingram M-10, minus the MAC suppressor. He lifted the SMG to spray a burst of .45 caliber hornets. Majors, pistol in hand, fired. Stiletto joined him and triggered a double-tap. The driver spun as slugs ripped through his upper body. He landed on his back in the center of the road.

Stiletto rose, breathing hard, the .45 gripped in both hands. He scanned the fallen bodies. Neither man moved.

"Good work," Stiletto said.

"Not a bad way to start the day."

They examined their car for damage. Other than a few dings, they'd avoided ruining the car.

"Come on," Majors said. They climbed back inside. Majors turned the car around to go back down the hill.

Stiletto sighed with satisfaction. Maybe the police murders would stop—for now. His mission was getting off to a great start. Who didn't feel good after killing drug thugs?

CHAPTER TWELVE

Majors drove to the safe house along a small side street lined with homes and apartment buildings. All had seen better days, with fading paint, and exteriors in need of repair. Debris littered the street. They were in a quiet neighborhood, but it didn't promise security. Stiletto knew all too well the nosy neighbors would take an interest in *gringos* going in and out.

"You sure this place is secure?" Stiletto said.

"We change locations tonight. Three days at each."

Kids up the street didn't seem to mind the condition of the neighborhood. They kicked a football back and forth to each other. Scott and Majors climbed out of the car. The front walkway of the safe house led to a narrow outdoor porch. Majors tapped a Morse code on the door before using his key. They entered. Majors had not exaggerated. The place was bare except for folding chairs around a poker table next to the kitchen.

Two other men, Ellis and McCoy, greeted them. Majors introduced Stiletto and Scott shook hands with both men. Like with Majors, he knew of them, but this was his first time meeting the pair.

McCoy was slim, blonde, bearded, with narrow shoulders. Ellis was shorter than the other three men by at least a foot, with his thinner hair clipped short.

"I don't like this location," Stiletto said. "Let's go over this extraction and get out of here."

McCoy led them to the poker table. Ellis opened a map. Scott noticed several red markings dotting the map. A glance at a corner of the room also showed two HK416 rifles propped in a corner.

"Which of these markings," Stiletto said, "is the Guardado spread?"

Majors pointed to one dot. "This is the hacienda, and this circle represents the entire ranch. Here's the road in and out."

"How many acres?"

Ellis said, "About 250."

"Mansion here, barracks here," Majors said. "There are some other buildings over here, smaller ones, along with the horse stables. Guardado's daughter rides."

"How many troops?"

"About one hundred," McCoy said. "They rotate with the troops who guard the processing plants and growing fields."

"Who gets me into the place?"

"Jackeline's bodyguard," Majors said. "Her name is Amaya Olmos. You'll meet her tonight at a restaurant we've picked out."

"When?"

Majors checked his watch. "In two hours."

Stiletto opened his mouth to reply, but what he wanted to say never passed his lips. A blast shook the house. The front door exploded inward. Stiletto and

Majors dove for cover while McCoy and Ellis ran for the HK416s.

———

Two gunmen in commando garb with submachine guns stormed through the smoke and debris from the blasted doorway.

They scanned for targets, but the masks over their faces limited their vision. Their pause was all Stiletto needed to shoot first. The Colt .45 in his fist cracked twice. One of the cartel killers dropped, almost colliding with his partner, who dodged, turning to fire as Majors bolted for the kitchen. Stiletto kicked over the poker table. The table would in no way stop a bullet, but the commando opened fire thinking Scott would hide there. Stiletto rolled away as the bullets chewed into the table-top. Ellis, one of the HKs at his shoulder, shot the invader in the head. The killer collapsed like a puppet with its strings cut.

McCoy and Ellis moved forward to check the bodies. Stiletto and Majors covered the room with their pistols.

"Anybody hit?" Scott said.

The three other Trust agents said they were okay.

Another blast shook the house. This one came from elsewhere. "Back bedroom!" Majors shouted.

McCoy and Ellis ran to the hallway across the room. They lined up on either side of the entry. Stiletto ducked behind the wrecked table. He and Majors had a clear view of the hallway and the three new cartel commandos moving in a staggered formation in the narrow space. Stiletto held up three fingers for Ellis and McCoy.

The lead commando fired at Scott, who fired twice in return. The first 230-grain Federal Hydra-Shok jacketed hollow-point closed the distance between Scott and his target at 1,000 feet per second. The bullet shattered the right knee of the lead commando. His kneecap split in half, spilling a spray of red onto the carpet. The man let out a yell as he toppled forward. The second bullet flew between the other two.

McCoy and Ellis swung their HKs into the hallway and fired on full auto. The two remaining killers jerked as the salvos stitched through them. The knee-shot gunner tried to raise his weapon, and Stiletto and Majors fired at the same time. Both slugs impacted with the gunner's head and added more gore to the mess.

"Clear!" Stiletto shouted.

"That was close," Majors said.

"We need to beat it," Stiletto said. "You guys got a car?" he said to Ellis and McCoy.

"In the garage," McCoy said.

"You three use that and get out of here. Mike, I'll take the car we came in."

Majors put away his gun and handed Stiletto the car keys. "We'll be in touch." He followed McCoy and Ellis to the garage.

"Send a picture of Amaya Olmos to my phone!" Stiletto yelled. Majors acknowledged.

Scott hustled out. He drove away wondering how the killers had known where to find them. But then he saw the kids were no longer playing in the street. Never mind nosy neighbors; the kids had done all the talking.

———

"Do you have to leave right away?"

Amaya Olmos lifted her head from the furry chest of Dante Costa. She didn't want to leave him or his bed any more than he did, but she'd only arranged the afternoon delight to see if he had any dirt on Manny Valdes.

She was following orders, after all, although she might have arranged the encounter anyway.

She placed her right hand on his chest and rested her chin. "Yes. It's business."

Dante shook his head. "Always business between us. And we'll both be at the hacienda, yet we can't spend any time together there."

She smiled. Partial wakefulness showed in her eyes. She figured she'd slept for an hour. "We have the same demanding employer." She sat up and swung a leg over one side of his naked body to straddle him. She didn't want to leave. With the recent stresses at the hacienda, her time with Dante had indeed been a nice distraction.

But she'd yet to ask about Manny Valdes's activity. Dante might have a lot to share—he was Manny's driver.

Amaya ran her fingers through the thick hair on Dante's chest.

"She's worried," Amaya said.

"She should be," he said. "Nobody knows where Carlos is."

Amaya moved her hands up and down his chest, trailed to his stomach. She felt him responding beneath her. "No. She's worried about Valdes."

"I'm concerned too."

"Why?"

"None of what I've seen him do lately has made sense. And then Carlos got captured. Mrs. Guardado probably needs to know."

"Tell me." She stopped, but let her fingernails linger on his skin.

"He's been driving himself lately."

"Not using you?"

"Yes. Like today."

"What did he say today?"

"He has business to do at home. He'll drive himself to the hacienda when he needs to check in."

"Where else has he been going and not using you as his driver?"

"I don't know where he's gone every time, but once I did follow him. You know how Carlos doesn't want anybody—"

"I get it." She grinded against him. "Tell me."

"I saw him meet a man in a parking lot. They spoke for five minutes. Valdes handed him an envelope."

"Who was the man?"

"No idea. Black hair, white suit, that's all I remember. I had no idea if he was on Guardado business or something else. And then Carlos—"

"That bastard!" Amaya hissed. She pulled free of Dante and rolled off the bed. She quickly picked up her discarded clothes, dropping them on the bed, and began to dress.

Dante sat up against the headboard. "You don't think Valdes—"

"I sure do," Amaya said. She busied herself with her clothes and didn't look at Dante. She wanted him to think she thought Valdes was responsible for what happened to Carlos, and might be planning more treachery. In reality, she only thought the second part. She zipped her jeans and talked in a rush. "He's never been content. He's always wanted to be in charge, but Carlos was in the way." She pulled a tank top over her bra and put on a T-shirt over both. She gathered her long hair and hurriedly tied it into a pony tail.

"But if he thinks he can simply kill Jackeline," she

continued, "and move in, he's wrong." She smoothed out the top.

"Why?"

"She has security measures. One being a tablet with all the secrets. The payoffs, codes, all that. If he doesn't get the tablet, he has nothing."

Last stop, the corner desk, where her pistol and holster lay. She hooked the holster behind her back.

"Hey," Dante said.

She turned to him, and a grin pulled at her mouth.

"What am I supposed to do with this?" He gestured at his erection.

"Hold your hat over it, darling," Amaya said. She blew him a kiss and went out.

Dante watched her go. When the door to his apartment closed, he reached for the phone on the night stand.

CHAPTER THIRTEEN

Amaya's "business" was meeting the American agent who'd get Jackeline and Sofia out of Colombia. But with a blue sedan on her tail, she had to arrive in one piece first.

She'd spotted the sedan as soon as she drove away from Dante's apartment, and the car had stayed with her. She'd driven a random pattern through the south side of Bogota to ascertain whether the car was truly following her or if she was being paranoid. The blue sedan stuck with her, attached like her nose, and she wasn't paranoid at all. Somebody *was* out to get her.

She drove through a housing tract, the road at a slight incline. Down the block, developers had left a patch of land open which included hills and scattered trees. If she had to face the goons in the sedan, the open space looked like a good battleground. She wanted to face them on her terms.

A glance in the rearview showed the sedan turning with her. No other cars on the road now. Only them. She slowed as she followed the curve of the road to the left, passing one of the hills, noting a number of deserted homes. Most of the occupants would be on their way home from work.

She stomped the gas pedal. The car lurched forward, tires screeching, as she finished the curve. She stopped alongside the hills with a large fallen tree trunk a welcoming piece of cover. Jumping from the car, she yanked her Beretta 92FS from the holster at her back. The nine-millimeter autoloader provided comfort as her shoes dug into the dirt. She ran to the fallen trunk.

The blue sedan screeched to a stop at the bottom of the hill. Two men climbed out carrying compact submachine guns. Amaya saw their hard looks and felt a twinge of doubt. Her pistol wasn't a match for full-auto hardware in the hands of determined killers.

Dante's description of Valdes's extracurricular dealings came back to her; she had a good idea who had sent the two converging on her. But where had he found them? She was certain they weren't Guardado troops. Had Valdes sent others to strike at Jackeline? Her pulse quickened. Valdes couldn't kill Jackeline without first getting rid of *her*.

If she survived, she'd learn the answers.

She had to survive, first.

Amaya dropped low and watched the two gunmen through a gap in the trunk. They began climbing, at a swift pace, in her direction.

One of the gunmen stumbled and fell to one knee, putting out a hand to break his fall. Amaya seized on the opportunity. She aimed her gun and fired twice. The sharp snaps of the rounds leaving the pistol echoed through the neighborhood. One bullet gouged the dirt near the gunman's hand, the second also a near miss based on how the man dove to get out of the way. Amaya fired again, her shot going wide as she tried to shift to the second shooter. The tree trunk blocked her from moving the muzzle where required. It might have been good cover but a lousy place to shoot from.

She moved fast, kicking up a small cloud of dust as she continued further up the hill. Another tree trunk to her left exploded as the gunners opened fire. The crackle of the submachine guns continued and she stumbled. Amaya fell headlong into the dirt, landing hard, and rolled down the opposite slope. Rocks dug into her skin and her body plowed over brush; branches and sharp thistles jabbed at her. She came to a sudden stop on her belly, hurting and gasping, but there was no time to rest. She crawled behind a bush, and realized during the roll she'd lost her pistol.

She looked up the slope and located the gun. The Beretta lay in the middle of an open patch of dirt waiting for somebody to pick it up. Amaya began to rise. The gunmen appeared over the top. She dropped down again. The gunmen spoke to each other rapidly, then split up. One found her Beretta and jammed it into his belt. He called to her, saying she should come out from hiding and "take it like a woman" but Amaya had no desire to surrender when her family was in jeopardy. She watched through the brush as the gunman started down the slope to her location.

She leaped out when he reached striking range and unleashed a series of kicks and punches, including an elbow thrust to the jaw. The gunner went down and out. She fell with him as his partner yelled, landing on her left side and using the man's larger body as a shield. Amaya grabbed his submachine gun. The second shooter ran toward them, his steps landing with loud thuds on the hard earth. She tucked the SMG's stock to her shoulder, lined up the sights, and put pressure on the trigger. The gunman stopped short, his eyes wide, and tried to raise his weapon. Too late.

The SMG in Amaya's hands spat flame. She kept the trigger back. The salvo split open the gunner's belly and spilled chunks of red flesh over the ground. The gunner dropped first to his knees, then toppled to one side. He slid along the slope till he came to a stop.

Gasping for breath, Amaya jumped to her feet. She tossed the empty SMG and retrieved the Beretta. She fired into the unconscious gunner's head, shuffling back to avoid the blood spray. Red spotted her shoes and pant legs anyway.

Amaya ran back up and over the hill, hustling to the car. She left a trail of rubber on the asphalt.

As she rejoined traffic, Amaya stole a glance at her watch, but had to wipe off dust to tell the time. She'd be late to her meeting, but didn't think the American would mind the delay once she explained. Dirt covered her clothes and her face and arms; she wouldn't have to explain very hard. She didn't mind the blood spatter on her pants, but she'd need a new pair of shoes for sure.

CHAPTER FOURTEEN

Valdes gripped the phone with white knuckles as he paced the room.

"What do you *mean* they didn't come back?"

He listened. He paced. He was at his apartment in the city, well away from the Guardado hacienda. The living room was well furnished, with rustic colors paramount. The voice on the other end of the line said:

"They haven't reported, and the police are responding to calls of a shooting and two dead."

"I paid you *well*," Valdes said. "You told me your men were up to the task."

Valdes had not recruited any Guardado loyalists to his side, true. But he knew people. He knew some nefarious types who would do the kind of work he required for a sizable amount of cash. To get rid of Jackeline he first needed to remove Amaya Olmos. Valdes had hired the two gunmen from the blue sedan via an intermediary, but now it appeared he'd wasted his time and money and Amaya Olmos still moved among the living.

"She was faster," the other man said.

Valdes cursed. He loosened his grip on the phone. He needed to calm down. A deep breath. He was glad he was such a neat freak and his place was spotless and free of clutter, otherwise he'd have been tempted to kick something across the room.

So much for his brilliant idea. Amaya would report the incident to Jackeline. She'd blame the phantom forces who had taken Carlos, which was the only silver lining. She wouldn't think about *him* ordering the killing. Then she'd increase security and complicate further attempts.

And he was running out of time.

"See to your dead," Valdes told the man on the phone. "Do not bother me again."

Valdes ended the call and tossed the cell phone on a chair. He turned to look through the open bedroom doorway. One of his regular hookers waited on his bed, but his call had taken priority. Esmerelda had dozed off during the conversation. She wore only stockings and lingerie barely concealed by a see-through wrap.

He went over to the bed and slapped the bottom of one foot. She awoke with a start. "That's not very nice!" she shouted. Esmerelda wiped her eyes. She raised an eyebrow at him. "Are you done with your boring talk? I've been waiting almost an hour." She sat up against the headboard and folded her arms. Her injected lips formed a bright red pout.

"I need help with my clothes," Valdes said.

What he really needed was some stress relief, and Esmerelda with her olive skin, fine curves and other attractions seemed like the best bet. She crawled across the bed to Valdes, rose to her knees, and reached for his belt.

———

Amaya Olmos drove past the restaurant, parked curbside around the corner, and returned on foot. She checked her phone as she entered, and told the hostess at the door she was meeting a friend. She detoured to the restroom.

She looked like a mess. Splashing water on her face and arms took care of most of the visible dirt, but there was nothing she could do about her clothes. She brushed them off with her hands as much as possible. She checked her phone again and memorized the face of Scott Stiletto, whom she was meeting per Mike Majors. Leaving the restroom, she began searching the restaurant. She ignored couples and groups. Stiletto would be sitting alone.

She found him at a small table in a corner. He sat with his back to the wall. She went over and said, "Are you the one I'm looking for?"

He locked eyes with her and she wanted to shrink away from his evaluation. He didn't consult his phone, so he'd either memorized her face or…what? Amaya found her thoughts scattered under the American's gaze.

"Depends," he said. "Are you looking for somebody who drinks—"

"Gin."

Stiletto held up his glass. Clear liquid and ice. "You guessed it." He smiled.

She joined him at the table.

He said, "That was one of the worst codes I've ever used. We get to blame it on Majors." He offered his hand. "I'm Scott."

"Amaya." They shook. A waiter appeared and she ordered tequila neat.

"You're late," he told her. "Any trouble getting here?"

"Yes," she said. "And I had to buy shoes."

"You *what*?"

"After I got blood on the ones I was wearing when two killers ambushed me."

"Better tell me what happened."

The waiter brought the tequila and Amaya drank half down in one swallow and ordered another. She began her story by relating her chat with Jackeline as they watched Sofia ride; she mentioned Manny Valdes, and her boyfriend Dante's story about his secret meetings. Stiletto listened without comment. She told of avoiding the two killers and how it made her late to the meeting. He nodded and swallowed more of his drink.

He said, "This operation has had its share of issues because of Manny Valdes."

"Yes," Amaya agreed. "He grabbed Beth. The woman you replaced. If she'd talked—"

"She didn't."

"If she had, the whole plan might be impossible to carry out."

Stiletto shook his head. "No it wouldn't."

"Do you know Beth?"

"She's a friend of mine, yes."

"I liked her. Is she okay?"

"I think so."

"I trust," she said, "you watch your back at all times?"

"It's why I'm sitting with the wall behind me. What happens when Valdes sees me at the ranch? If he was suspicious of one American hanging around, he might—"

This time she smiled. "Shit a brick."

"It'll be the last one he shits," Stiletto said. "I'm supposed to punch his ticket before we leave."

"If I don't kill him first."

"If he sent men after you, what about Jackeline?"

"I called and told her. She's safe. Valdes can't do anything without getting rid of me first."

"Fair enough. Let's talk about what your boyfriend saw. What do you think Valdes has in mind?"

"With Carlos gone, he wants to move in."

"But it sounds like he had a plan in mind *before* we grabbed Carlos."

"If I didn't know the whole story," Amaya said, "I'd suggest he engineered Carlos's capture. I mean—"

"I understand what you mean."

She nodded and drank another mouthful of tequila, finishing the glass. The waiter brought her second right on cue.

"If he's planning something," Stiletto said once the waiter had gone, "he'd need help. Who might he reach out to?"

"The same people he sent after me. Thugs. Hired killers."

"You sure they were hired?"

"They weren't Guardado people, I know for sure. He *might* try for an alliance—"

"With another cartel?"

"It's possible."

"And he might have people at the hacienda now."

She agreed.

"What it means is we need to get Jackeline and Sofia out faster than we expected. Does this exit include you?"

"I suppose."

"Can you take me to Jackeline now?"

Amaya grabbed her tequila and downed the contents of the glass. She told Stiletto to finish his drink. "My car's around the corner," she added.

Stiletto left his unfinished drink behind and money on the table.

CHAPTER FIFTEEN

With Esmerelda gone, Manny Valdes had more business to take care of. He wore a bathrobe and once again paced the floor while on the phone. This time, he spoke with Jorge Ramirez.

"They'll be on alert now," Ramirez said. "Your attempt may have—"

"It hasn't ruined anything," Valdes snapped. "In fact, it helps our position."

"How?" the older cartel kingpin asked.

"Amaya will run to Jackeline, back to the hacienda."

"Where they will increase security."

"And be right where we want them. I will go there too, and I can take care of our business. We can have control by morning."

"You can't kill the woman."

Valdes blinked. "What?"

"We've learned some new information. Are you aware of a tablet computer on which Jackeline Guardado keeps information on payoffs and other secrets?"

Valdes frowned. "I am not."

"We need it. We need to know who the Guardado's have in their pocket. The transition must be seamless. If they're paying certain people, we need to maintain the payoffs otherwise they will pose a risk."

"I'm going to need help then," Valdes said.

"What do you suggest?"

"I'm going to need an army. Full assault on the hacienda. I'll get to the woman and her precious computer during the fight."

"Using such resources requires discussion. I need to talk with Sanchez."

"Of course."

"Report when you arrive and have an idea of the security precautions."

"We'll talk soon," Valdes said.

He ended the call and tossed the cell on the bed. Time for a shower, then a drive to the hacienda. He headed for his bathroom.

———

Sofia Guardado wanted to get out of the house.

But she had to make sure her mother didn't catch her.

She sat in front of her vanity brushing her hair and hating her chin. Everything else she had she gained from her mother, but DNA provided her father's chin and it jutted out like a chisel. If she put on 300 pounds it might vanish, but who wanted to gain 300 pounds?

Whatever. Her chin was her chin. Her boyfriend Juan didn't seem to mind. She combed her hair some more, one side then the other, and decided to think of Juan rather than her chin. She had to sneak out to see him. The ranch was on lockdown—because of her father. She was worried about him and what might happen to her and her mother now. Were they next? She needed a break. A few hours with Juan would make her feel better.

She finished her hair. It looked rich and long and silky. She wanted to wear something nicer than jeans and a T-shirt but going over the wall made a dress out of the question. The night was warm, but she left the dresses in the closet.

A knock at the door. "Sofia!"

Her mother.

Jackeline tried the knob. It didn't turn.

"Open the door, Sofia. *Now.*"

What the hell was she yelling about?

Sofia let out a frustrated breath and slumped her shoulders. So much for her escape. Leaving the vanity, she flicked the lock on the door. Her mother pushed the door open before Sofia turned the knob.

"Why is the door locked?"

"Privacy? Is that a crime? We got scary guys running all over the house, Mom!"

"Where are you going?"

"*What?*"

"Don't *what* me, young lady. We caught Juan on the perimeter. He's lucky he wasn't shot."

"Oh my *gawd*, Mom!"

"You need to stay here, Sofia. It's too dangerous right now."

"Can't I go out for an hour?"

"You were going to be gone longer than an hour, Sofia."

"What did you do to Juan?"

"He's driving home. I asked him some questions and he answered me and I sent him home."

Sofia folded her arms. She had the same habit as her mother, putting her hands on her hips when she was upset, and worked hard not to duplicate the habit too much.

"What the hell is going on, Mom?"

"Watch your mouth."

"What's going on with Daddy?"

Jackeline's voice softened. "We still don't know, honey."

"So, what, I'm supposed to stay in my room?"

"You can go anywhere you want but don't leave the house."

"Seriously?"

"If you're caught trying to sneak out, there will be consequences, Sofia."

"Fine!"

Sofia turned from the door and jumped onto her bed. She folded her arms again and pouted. She glared at her mother. Jackeline glared back.

Sofia said, "Are you *done*?"

"We'll be back to normal in a few days, Sofia. Won't be long."

"Where have I heard *that* before? Only two weeks!"

Jackeline pulled the door shut. Sofia wondered if she could go out and see her horse, or if *bitch tits* would throw another fit.

———

Jackeline pulled Sofia's door shut. She went down the hall to a pair of glass doors, and stepped out onto the east balcony. The warm night felt good. The lights outside were low; two of her gunners, submachine guns cradled loosely, stood nearby.

"Mrs. Guardado—" one began.

"I need fresh air."

"Ma'am—"

"Give me two minutes. There's nowhere out there for anybody to hide anyway."

Well, so she assumed. On the eastern side of the hacienda, they'd long ago cleared the trees and brush and planted grass. The flat land was mined and strewn with razor wire. Any sniper who passed through the security measures deserved a chance to take a shot at her.

Jackeline stayed out of the pool of light and allowed the two gunners to stand at the balcony rail, effectively shielding her.

Back to normal?

Bullshit.

Sofia had no idea what was really going on. She couldn't count on the teenager not blabbing to her boyfriend, who would then tell his father, who was yet another member of the cartel fraternity. She hated to cause Sofia pain, but at least Jackeline knew the truth—it wouldn't last long, but what their life might look like after, she had no clue. Sofia's father was fine, perfectly safe, and she'd be reunited with him soon.

As long as the two of them escaped in one piece. With the help of Amaya and the American she had yet to meet, she figured their odds of getting away about fifty-fifty. She'd revise her opinion as time went on. There were still variables to consider. Still Valdes to deal with. She'd taken Amaya's report without comment, because it didn't matter what he was engineering. They'd be gone soon, and he'd be left with a bullet in his head. Nothing he had cooked up within his scheming mind would *ever* come to pass.

Jackeline checked her watch. Amaya was bringing the American; she'd arrive soon.

She cursed under her breath. The whole situation

might have been better had the four of them—she wasn't going to leave Amaya behind—escaped at the same time. But appearances were important if they wanted to remain free of reprisals. The other cartels would want them dead once they realized what happened. They also had to get rid of Valdes, who would never stop trying to solve the mystery behind their departure. Somebody would learn the truth, but Jackeline planned to be well out of public view, her family safe, when the information finally surfaced. Because once she and Sofia were out, Jackeline would play her ace. She'd expose many government officials in Colombia *and* the United States for their corruption and cooperation with the cartels. They'd all get their comeuppance. They'd all know where the kill shot came from.

Jackeline wanted to atone for her sins and protect her daughter. Once the ace was deployed, she'd accomplish all of her goals at one time.

The anticipation made the wait almost worthwhile.

Almost.

CHAPTER SIXTEEN

Stiletto held his cell to his ear as Mike Majors spoke.

"We are at the extraction site. Standing by for your arrival."

"Copy," Scott said into the phone. "I'm with Amaya on our way to the ranch."

"Watch your back."

"Back, front, and every other angle I can think of," Stiletto said. "I'll shout when we're on route."

Stiletto hung up and returned the phone to his jacket pocket.

Amaya said, "I wish the sun was still out."

"It's fine," he said.

They'd left the city limits fifteen minutes earlier and now traveled a curvy mountain road north of the city. The route gave Scott a sense of déjà vu—but it was a different road than the one he and Majors had chased the cop killers on only a few hours earlier.

The car's headlamps carved the way ahead, the tarmac smooth, nothing but dense jungle on either side.

Amaya negotiated the curves with ease. She'd made the drive countless times before.

"It's nice here," she said. "You know, when people aren't getting murdered in the streets."

Scott didn't reply, but it surprised him somebody who was responsible for some of those murders, directly or not, would have her perspective.

He'd seen enough of the natural scenery to at least agree with her main point. Many countries experiencing violent strife were nice, or had areas to recommend. Violence and dirty warfare kept guys like Stiletto—and, ultimately, people like Amaya too—in business. The day world peace broke out, Scott had better have another way to support himself. But he wasn't worried. As long as nations with different values, cultures, experiences, and expectations existed, conflict was all but assured.

Stiletto shifted in his seat as Amaya continued up the mountain road.

What would he do if he ever left the shadow world?

He'd told Dr. Gargarin he had no idea what to do with himself if he wasn't working. And by "working" he meant going into harm's way on a regular basis.

He thought about Ali Lewis in San Francisco and Kim Jordan in Seattle. Previous women in his life, both of whom ran successful businesses. Both had extended offers for him to work for them. Ali Lewis ran a clothing company and wanted Scott's expertise as an artist to draw new designs. Kim Jordan was CEO of a defense firm and wanted Scott as a security consultant. He'd been in love with both once, but he was drawn to the kind of action neither woman could provide. He didn't know how to leave. If world peace forced his retirement, fine. But until an outside force played its hands, he'd remain in the shadow world.

There was still a lot to do to make the world a better place, and maybe if he did his job well enough, there might be an era where warriors weren't needed any longer.

He could hope.

He shook his head to clear the train of thought. Time to change the topic and get his thoughts turned to something, or someone, else.

Scott said to Amaya, "How did you become Jackeline's bodyguard?"

Amaya slowed for a right turn, eased the wheel left when the curve changed direction, and straightened the wheels.

"I grew up in Chile," she said. "My parents were active in various guerilla groups. When other kids were riding bicycles, I was slinging det cord."

"Fun times."

"It was all fun and games but for the occasional blown-off hand or finger."

Another comment Scott decided not to respond to.

"Eventually all the anarchist and anti-capitalist guerillas went inactive—well, sort of."

Stiletto stifled a chuckle.

"And," she continued, "I drifted into working for the cartels. Eventually I met Carlos and Jackeline and she made me her bodyguard. Then we became close friends."

"Why did she pick you?"

Amaya scoffed. "Why do you think? Rape insurance. Murder insurance. I didn't grow up in the cartels so I have no loyalty to them. Or designs on Jackeline's position. My loyalty is to the people I love, and the family I've chosen after losing my own."

"What happened to your family?"

"I do not care to discuss it."

Stiletto nodded. The ride continued. He let the silence remain between them. He had a feeling Amaya Olmos had done all the talking she cared to do for the time being.

But he was wrong.

"There is something you need to know," she said.

"What?"

She explained the conversation between Jackeline and Valdes regarding a strike back; how Jackeline ordered Valdes to have their people look for American drug agents.

"One of our people on the street—"

"Let me guess," Stiletto said. "Kids playing football, a safe house in a quiet neighborhood. Yeah, I was there, Amaya. Had it gone the other way, you and your friends wouldn't have a way out of this shithole country. Get it?"

"Don't get mad at me."

"I'll save it for your boss, don't worry."

"Maybe I shouldn't have told you."

"I *might* have figured it out after a while."

This time, Amaya remained quiet.

———

Jackeline Guardado stuffed the last cartridge into the 30-round magazine and rocked it into the magwell of her Kalashnikov.

Her pink AK-47. A ridiculous weapon. She'd loved everything about the weapon when she was twenty-one, but her youth was far in the rearview mirror.

Or so she told herself. Early forties actually weren't terrible after all, though her weight fluctuated more than she cared for. She set the automatic rifle in a corner near her bed. The magazine had a second mag attached via a "jungle clip." Sixty rounds of steel-tipped 7.62x39mm to start. She had a shoulder bag full of more magazines which she kept next to the rifle.

Jackeline stayed well back from the bedroom balcony facing the north, but stared into the night beyond the balcony rail with her arms folded. She'd come a long way to this moment, and didn't stop the flood of memories coming through her mind.

Her dual citizenship in the United States was something nobody ever dwelled on. Her mother and father were visiting relatives in Seattle when Jackeline demanded release from the womb. Her parents never admitted they made the trip to make sure she was born in the US, nor did they ever admit to grooming her for the drug business, but her father grew opium poppy for the Guardado Cartel, and her ability to come and go from the US had helped her father's end of the business while she was growing up, so she figured their trickery was obvious.

The Guardado leadership were common guests at her house. The cartel, at the time, was led by Carlos's father, Javier. It was through those family connections that Jackeline and Carlos eventually met. They didn't date until they were teenagers. Her parents and his encouraged the relationship. The pressure Jackeline felt to go with Carlos wasn't fun. She wasn't sure she'd like the guy, and then what? But he was such a charmer he won her over. After they fell in love, she'd needed no further encouragement from her parents.

But it wasn't all straight-and-narrow for Jackeline, or at least the cartel version of straight-and-narrow. Jackeline trained for a short time with a group of *sicarias* when she was nineteen. They'd been young women picked to form an assassination squad to target rivals and cops via any means. Guns, knives, bombs, sex—nothing was off the table or discouraged. Carlos didn't want her in the group, but it would be at least a year before he had the power to pull her away. In the meantime, Jackeline acquired her pink AK-47 and the skills to use the weapon with great effect.

When Carlos's father died, the son took over. First act: get Jackeline away from the *sicarias*. Several girls from her group had already died in retaliation killings, or from police bullets. She joined him at the Guardado hacienda, where they married. Second act: make Jackeline his number two in the organization.

In the male-dominated world of the cartels, it wasn't impossible for women to hold positions of power, but never before had the wife of a cartel boss had as much power as Jackeline. Cartel wives were expected to remain behind the scenes, never at the front of an operation. They were supposed to remain submissive to their husbands' needs, take care of the kids, and look the other way when their husbands fooled around with mistresses. Carlos Guardado broke the mold and made a lot of people angry in the process. They'd both lived with targets on their backs, but managed to survive and thrive. When Sofia came along, everything changed.

Jackeline vividly recalled the moment she snapped a picture of Sofia, at five years of age, covered in a pile of American dollars. What had started as a cute picture instead became a moment of clarity Jackeline had never foreseen.

She couldn't allow Sofia to grow up the way she had.

Cartel life was no place for children, despite how many babies her contemporaries produced. She wanted to get her daughter out by any means necessary.

It wasn't hard to convince Carlos of the need to make a change.

But *nobody* simply walked away from the drug world.

They had to find a way to get clear and keep their lives intact. Keep Sofia safe. Going to the DEA or CIA was out of the question; another "no way" was to approach the Colombian government. Jackeline's files were full of dossiers on corrupt officials in both countries, most of whom were on the Guardado payroll. To ask them to see her family to the United States in exchange for information meant their lives, the exact opposite of what they wanted.

A few months went by, and they watched Sofia approach her sixth birthday. Their desperation for a solution grew with her. Carlos and Jackeline began hearing rumors of an organization called The Trust. The private intelligence organization, not tied to any government or hip deep in corruption, seemed like their best bet. Carlos dispatched agents to learn about The Trust, and they came back with enough information for Carlos and Jackeline to make an attempt to contact the group.

The Trust agreed to the proposition with the caveat they wait at least five years, and feed information in the meantime.

There was another problem, though.

The Trust, with no legal standing in the US, could not offer any true witness protection, immunity, anything to make sure the Guardados made a safe transition to the US. All they promised was to get them into the country, and provide new identities. The rest would be up to them.

Carlos and Jackeline passed information to their contacts while working on the plan for after. Jackeline's dual citizenship once again came in handy.

During the waiting period, Jackeline traveled to the US several times. Each trip, she brought money. Cash. Gold bars. The cash went into private accounts; the gold Jackeline buried. All they had to do was get into the US. The Trust promised transport and new identities. Once there, they'd have enough money to live and hide out wherever they wanted.

But it all meant nothing if Jackeline and Sofia didn't reach the US alive.

She had to deal with Manny Valdes and anybody working with him to make sure they escaped.

CHAPTER SEVENTEEN

The buzz of her bedroom intercom jarred Jackeline from her thoughts. She crossed to the closed bedroom door and the intercom speaker beside the frame. She pressed the Talk button.

"What is it?"

"Ms. Olmos has arrived," the gate guard said. "She has a man with her and claims you're expecting him, ma'am."

She didn't recognize the voice of the gate guard, but she was glad her people were taking her increased security edict to heart.

"I am expecting this man," she said. "Let them through. Tell Ms. Olmos I will meet her at the front door and she is to wait for me."

"Yes, ma'am."

Jackeline released the button and gave herself one final look in the bathroom mirror. She didn't care about her overall appearance, but she wanted to check her face. She had to look strong. She had to keep her people assured all was well despite the crisis. But she realized, after darting from her own gaze, she wanted the American to believe the same thing.

———

Amaya eased the car through the front gate. She followed the access road toward the house. It was a one-lane road. The exit side was on their left, with a large fountain in between at the midway point. Four weeping angel statues surrounded the water spout in the center. Small lights in the lawn shined on the fountain.

The evening twilight gave the property a low glow. There weren't any other lights, except a few on the outside of the mansion to light walkways. Stiletto spotted flashlights out in the field. Troops patrolling the inner perimeter.

The road curved again in front of the main entrance. Amaya pulled off and stopped a few feet from the porch steps.

Four men with Heckler & Koch submachine guns approached the car. Their eyes settled on Stiletto. They looked like hungry lions but on two legs and holding guns.

"Don't worry about them," Amaya said. She opened the car door and climbed out. She shut the door and spoke to the troops. Stiletto exited and stood beside the car. Amaya finished talking and the troops returned to their stations around the front. They never stopped looking mean, ready to kill.

Amaya came over to him. "Everybody's uptight."

"Tell me about it."

"Once one of them sees you with Jackeline, they won't be so ferocious."

"Uh-huh."

She smiled. "You can relax."

"Can I?"

Stiletto forced a smile. Amaya received the unspoken message and stopped talking.

He could not relax in the current environment. He was in a pit of vipers. They were people responsible for innumerable deaths, lives of misery, and they made billions doing so. Their ilk had supplied the drugs on which his niece overdosed. His brother's family always had an empty seat at the holiday table. He found himself fantasizing about murdering every breathing human on the property.

Starting with Amaya. Poor little sob story be damned.

But orders were orders. He'd made a commitment to General Fleming, and to Mike Majors, who had more time invested in the project than he. He had to go through with it for Beth Carrington, if nothing else, because she'd invested in the mission as well. It wasn't fair to his teammates if he sabotaged the mission out of revenge for an incident where no matter how many he killed, his niece wasn't coming back.

The front door opened and the porch light snapped on. The bright light revealed thick marble columns holding up the overhang of the roof. They also highlighted a statuesque woman making her way to him.

———

Stiletto hated doing a double-take but if Jackeline Guardado had been anything other than a cartel queen, she'd be collecting double-takes wherever she went.

Tall, long-legged and curvy with an oversize blouse still failing to hide anything she might want to downplay, Jackeline Guardado didn't smile as she reached Scott and

Amaya. Instead, she opened with, "You didn't get killed or captured. Very good."

"No thanks to you," Stiletto said.

"Your name?"

"Stiletto. Scott Stiletto."

"Are you a shoe salesman in your spare time?"

"As long as there are people like you in the world, I'll never need a side gig."

She put her hands on her hips. "You think you're funny?"

"I think, Mrs. Guardado, you and I need to talk inside. Away from your people."

"Nobody makes decisions around here except me."

"Of course," Scott said. "Let's go inside."

Amaya finally said, "Enough, Jackie, you made your point."

Jackeline shot Amaya a quick glance, lowered her arms to her sides, and marched back into the house. Scott and Amaya followed. Stiletto watched Jackeline walk and decided she was more interesting from the front than the rear.

———

Sofia watched her mother talk to Aunt Amaya and the unknown man. She saw them from the window of her bedroom which overlooked the front of the house. The way her mother put her hands on her hips meant she wasn't happy, and she wondered what they were saying to each other. He looked American. Had he brought news about her father?

She turned away from the window. They'd go to her mother's office. There was no way to sneak up there and eavesdrop, but it did mean her mother would be busy for a while. Maybe she and Juan might...

Sofia hurried to her vanity where she'd put her cell phone. She fired a text to Juan.

S: *Heard you got busted.*

J: *Your Mom is freaked.*

S: *Duh you heard about my Dad.*

J: *Are you at home?*

S: *Yeah and she's busy so you wanna try again?*

J: *No.*

S: *WHAT???*

J: *She's gonna kill me.*

S: *She was just trying to scare you.*

J: *No way not doing it let's wait.*

S: *You ass.*

J: *I wanna keep my ass!*

S: *Then you get no more of mine till you become a man. Bye!*

J: *Wait.*

She didn't respond.

J: *Sofia? Come on!*

Sofia turned off notifications from Juan's number and put her phone down. She'd let him stew for a while and try again later. Much later. Once everybody was asleep and the guards who remained awake weren't paying as much attention.

———

Stiletto frowned as the three of them walked into Jackeline's office. Bright colors and knickknacks; red and green lamps, matching furniture, the ubiquitous large desk. Jackeline led them to the couches and told Amaya to get drinks. Scott asked for a gin and tonic with a slice of lime.

Stiletto and Jackeline had a staring contest as Amaya prepared the drinks. The bodyguard brought the glasses on a tray. Scott took his drink. Amaya handed Jackeline a glass of red wine, and she'd poured a similar glass for herself. When Amaya finally sat across the coffee table from Scott, Jackeline spoke.

"What's the plan for getting us out?"

"No," Stiletto said. "What's the deal with sending killers to our safe house?"

Jackeline explained her rationale, repeating much of what Amaya had told him. *At least they're consistent.*

"I tried to send a warning," she said.

"We didn't get it. You didn't try very hard."

"It was necessary to keep up—"

"If we'd been killed, you'd be hitchhiking to the United States." Stiletto drank some gin and tonic. "Or tagging along with one of those immigrant caravans. Wouldn't that be fun?" To Amaya he said, "Nice mix."

Amaya gave him half a grin in return.

Jackeline said, "I will pay you and your team a bonus to make up for the unfortunate incident at the house."

Stiletto laughed. "Sure."

"You don't like me."

"No, I don't. I lost a niece because of people like you."

"I'm sorry."

"Are you?"

"My husband and I have come to regret everything we've done."

"Because of your daughter."

"Yes. Children change you."

"I know."

She paused to drink some wine and Stiletto decided he needed to cool down and back off. She seemed genuine, and he knew what leading a double life might do to somebody. People trying to be one person while behaving like another felt an immense psychological pressure, which affected one physically as well. But she hadn't appeared to have lost any sleep recently. Maybe she knew how to handle the pressure better than most.

Play nice. She can help destroy the other cartels.

"All right," Stiletto said. "We know where each of us stands. You want to get to your husband. It's my job to get you there."

"Yes. What is the plan?"

"My team is standing by a few miles from here. All we need to do is take care of Manny Valdes, and we can go."

"He's not here."

"Will that change?" Scott said.

"Soon."

"Can we deal with him quietly?"

"It's a big ranch, and yes. I have some questions for him before you kill him, though. He has a lot to answer for."

"Okay. When the time comes, the four of us will make our move. What about any compatriots Valdes might have? Will removing him put them out of action?"

"Whatever he is planning," Jackeline said, "will fall apart with his demise. Whoever he's connected with might be *outside* the cartel."

"Could be."

Stiletto sighed and pressed his lips together.

"You don't think—"

Stiletto held up a hand and she stopped talking. "I wish we knew a little more," he explained. "I don't think he's a major cog in whatever the plan might be. He's the inside man for somebody else."

"We can talk in circles all you want, Mr. Stiletto, but kill Valdes and it's over. He cannot live to track down my husband, me, or my daughter."

Stiletto nodded.

Jackeline checked her watch. "It's a quarter after seven. What are you thinking for a timeline?"

"Five, six more hours," he said, "if Valdes shows up. If you can, get some rest. It will be a long night no matter what we do."

"Who can sleep?" Jackeline said.

Stiletto admitted he wasn't sure he could either.

CHAPTER EIGHTEEN

Dante Costa, Amaya's "suitor" or whatever she called it, as not even *he* had any idea of how to define their relationship other than occasional lovers, knew about her arrival within ten minutes. Everybody was talking about the American, who he might be, and what his presence at the hacienda meant.

When he wasn't driving Manny Valdes, Costa worked in the garage taking care of Carlos and Jackeline's cars. The lady boss had told him she wanted her Mercedes S-Class cleaned and checked out and ready for travel. He'd already changed the oil and topped off other fluids, and now had the wheels and tires off to inspect the brakes.

Dante had to focus because a rush of thoughts battled through his mind. He knew the American was connected to the Carlos situation. He needed to let Ramirez know quickly but didn't dare try to contact him while on the property. He never knew who might be listening around a corner, out of sight, but able to hear.

He shined a flashlight into the brake hub to look at

the thickness of the brake pad and condition of the rotor. He saw no issues.

The tablet. The *tablet*. All he wanted was to get his hands on Jackeline's tablet. Ramirez would reward him handsomely. But how to do so?

He'd called the aging cartel boss to deliver the new information after Amaya had left his apartment. Ever since, he'd been wondering how to acquire the device. He needed Amaya. She was the only one who could get him close enough. But how to get Amaya to help was the question. She wasn't a pushover or somebody easily blackmailed.

Or...

He moved from the front passenger brake to the rear and shined his light again. He had an idea, and it was staring him in the face as he worked. All he had to do was wait for Jackeline to require the car. Who else would drive but him? He'd have Jackeline and Amaya and Sofia in one place. A little pressure on the daughter and Jackeline would crack. He might have to kill Amaya, but the reward coming his way would make up for the loss. She didn't mean much anyway; she was a quick screw now and then.

He continued with his task as the plan took further shape, and quieted his mind. All he had to do was wait.

––––––––

Amaya led Stiletto down a hallway. He might have been walking the hall of the finest hotel in Paris or New York City. Thick carpet, blue, with square designs at three-inch intervals, wood paneled walls, none of the décor cheap. Carved pieces of wood lined the upper corners of the hall; wooden wainscoting for the lower portion. For "guest quarters" it was first class. And then he remembered how Jackeline and her husband paid for the extravagance of the interior design. Blood money. His features looked grim as Amaya stopped at a door and inserted a keycard into the slot above the doorknob.

"Very nice," Stiletto remarked. He tried not to make it sound like an insult.

The smirk she gave in return suggested she knew he was trying hard to remain cordial.

"Try not to get too comfortable," she said.

"We won't be here long, yeah."

Stiletto looked around. The hotel motif continued. Bed, flat screen—the usual. Every piece in the room, from bed to dresser to walk-in shower, showed top quality material.

"How do I reach you?" he asked.

"I'm two doors down. Use the phone. Pound two-four-seven."

"Don't you mean *hashtag*? I didn't know kids your age recognized the pound sign."

"I'm not as young as I look." She handed him the keycard and left. He turned the lock.

Scott crossed to the drapes and pulled them aside. He stared out at an open field. It was too dark to identify anything specific.

He turned from the window and reached for his cell phone. He figured Jackeline's people had bugged the room, but so what? She was one of the good guys now, right?

He scoffed and dialed General Fleming.

"Status?" the General said after they exchanged greetings.

"We've met."

"Are you being good?"

"I'm following orders, sir."

"Acceptable."

"Are you aware the bodyguard is coming with us?"

"Whatever it takes to keep Jackeline Guardado happy is fine."

"Sir, I'm curious. What's the plan when they get to the States? It's not like we can put them in WITSEC."

"We'll get there. For now, say it's complicated. If they ask."

"She hasn't. I think they've made a private arrangement."

"As long as they deliver what they promised, we'll work with them."

"What have they promised?" Stiletto said.

"Ask her yourself. Hearing it from Jackeline might make you feel better."

"I will, sir."

"What else is on your mind?"

"We talked about a couple things on our last call."

"Beth is doing well. She's awake and responding to treatment. Little rehab and she'll be fine. Couple months at most."

"And our hacker friend?"

"We're almost done but the other team is still asking for a crack at him. We're mulling it over."

"I don't like the idea of giving those jerks on the other team any help, sir."

"You're not alone."

"All right. I need a nap. We move out in a few hours."

"Good luck and be careful."

"Will do." Stiletto hung up and made a second call to Mike Majors at the extraction site. He gave the update and stuck to basics. He didn't want to keep Majors talking too long.

Stretching out on the bed, he sank into the soft pillow top and down comforter. Whatever information Jackeline and her husband promised to hand over had better be dynamite, he decided. He quickly dozed off.

———

Amaya Olmos turned on the bathroom light in her room and leaned against the counter. She looked at her dirty face in the mirror and went to turn on the shower. As the water warmed, she stripped off her clothes. Dust fell from her shirt and jeans as she dropped them on the floor. As always, she ignored the scrawny figure in the mirror. She didn't like to look at herself. All she ever saw was droopy fried-egg breasts and bony hips, and the scar tissue decorating her body. She had enough scars, inside and out, to last a lifetime.

Amaya sighed as she stepped under the hot spray and began to soap away the dried sweat and dirt. She'd feel human again in no time.

She had no idea what the future held, but it had to be better than where she was now.

———

Mike Majors loved the sound of chirping crickets.

Chirping crickets meant the enemy wasn't sneaking up on you.

He listened to Stiletto's update and acknowledged the timeline. He told McCoy and Ellis, and the pair returned to their guard positions.

The three men were spread out over a small camp with an off-roader aimed at the dirt road Majors marked as their exit. The humid jungle surrounding them held more critters than only crickets, but critters weren't on the team's list of concerns. They wanted to avoid creatures of the two-legged variety. Majors, McCoy, and Ellis had their watch positions, but they'd also set up an electronic perimeter. Sensors hidden at twenty-five and fifty meters, 360 degrees, would activate alerts on their watches. If the sensors failed, the crickets were backup.

Mike Majors shifted his angle of view. He'd been laying prone for half an hour, enjoying the cover of the foliage. His HK416 was ever-present and ready to fire. Only a few more hours. Stiletto promised to call when he was on the move with the women.

Only a few more hours...

The crickets continued to chirp.

CHAPTER NINETEEN

Manny Valdes stopped at the gate. The overhead lamps on the guard house roof highlighted his face behind the driver's side window glass. He didn't lower the window. The guard also didn't leave his seat. He pressed a button to open the gate and Valdes drove through.

Valdes grimaced. If she was going for minimum light around the place, why leave the fountain lights on? He drove by the fixture. Valdes wanted to talk to the chief house guard before doing anything else. He had to know how many extra troops were on the grounds. Then he had to update Ramirez and figure out how to separate Jackeline from the tablet. Dammit, why was he only learning of the thing *now* after all his years of service? What else had Carlos and *the woman* held back?

He stopped the car at the front of the house. The man at the gate must have phoned ahead because the chief house guard waited on the porch steps. Valdes handed his keys to the *sicario* who held his door for him, and the much younger shooter drove the car to the garage.

"You're the man I'm looking for, Xavier."

Valdes joined Xavier on the porch. The bulky house chief stood a few inches shorter, but Valdes felt the power coming from the smaller man. He wore a pistol on his hip, and his rough face and hands told all who glanced his way he was somebody with the ability to alter or end their life *without* the handgun.

"What may I help you with, Mr. Valdes?"

"How many troops are here?"

"Same amount as always."

"What?"

"Mrs. Guardado does not want to leave anything without proper protection."

"Not even freelancers to bulk up the ranch?"

"She does not trust freelancers, Mr. Valdes."

"Right. It's obvious you consider—" Valdes stopped. He was letting Xavier and his hard stare disrupt him. "I need to see her."

"Mrs. Guardado has asked not to be disturbed."

"It's important she and I talk."

Xavier shook his head.

"Where is Olmos?" Valdes asked.

"Ms. Olmos is not to be disturbed, Mr. Valdes."

"What's going on around here?"

Xavier shrugged. "I have my instructions."

Valdes let out a sigh. If he was going to learn anything more, he needed to see the troops. As overall commander of Guardado forces, Xavier had no authority to stop him from inspecting their posts.

"I'm going to talk to the troops," he said. "When I return, I expect she will see me."

Xavier said okay, and returned to his post inside the house. Valdes began his interviews with the gunners working the front. He learned about the presence of the American right away.

———

Forty minutes later, Valdes completed his check of the perimeter security positions. The roving patrols he didn't worry about.

He walked deep into the shadows on the west side of the property, where the trees were thickest, and found a secluded spot. If any patrol found him, there'd be no question why he was there alone. He dialed Ramirez and held the smartphone to his ear.

"What is it?" the older cartel boss said.

"We have a problem."

Before Ramirez questioned him further, Valdes told him what he knew about the mysterious American and how *the woman* had sealed herself from contact.

Ramirez remained quiet once Valdes finished his report. Valdes waited. The silence lasted a few moments.

"What do you think this visit means?" Ramirez said. "Why a second American?"

Valdes raised an eyebrow. He'd expected Ramirez to blow a gasket; instead, he spoke soberly, without any anger.

"I have one conclusion," Valdes said. "The Americans took Carlos. The woman we captured was some kind of advance scout."

"But what does it *mean*, Valdes?"

"Carlos has cracked under interrogation. He wants to make a deal. He'll trade information for his family and witness protection."

"I see."

"They can undo—"

"I'm aware of the damage they can cause, Valdes."

"Another thing occurred to me," Valdes said. "What if

our troubles of late have come from Carlos the whole time?"

"It would suggest his *capture* was a ploy."

"Exactly. And the American is here to evacuate mother and daughter."

"It's far-fetched, Valdes."

"What we *do* know is there is an American here, and we don't have any more time."

"We are organizing our forces," Ramirez said. "When they strike, you will kill Jackeline and the bodyguard and obtain the tablet. Do whatever you want with the daughter."

"I'd expect a development either in the next few hours or by morning. Can your people be ready?"

"It will take us two hours."

"This will be our only chance," Valdes said.

"The tablet is more important than the daughter, Valdes. Keep that in mind."

"I'll *get* the tablet. But I *need* your forces."

"You'll have them. Stand by."

Ramirez hung up. Valdes put away his phone and wiped his face with a handkerchief. He hadn't been aware he was sweating. And he was also trembling.

So close.

His dream was about to become reality.

———

Stiletto rolled over and woke up. He'd only slept an hour, and after trying to drift off again over the next thirty minutes, gave up. He rolled onto his back and supported his head with his right hand. He contemplated the ceiling and let his thoughts wander.

He was in the midst of a powerful enemy. One he had

to *help*. Orders or not, the objective made his gut turn over. No wonder he couldn't sleep. He thought of his niece, Bailey Rose, the young girl he'd tried to avenge long ago. What had those killings achieved? Another drug crew replaced the one he wiped out. The cycle continued. He applied the same thoughts to all the other enemies he'd faced in a career of constant violence. No problems were solved for long. Kill one enemy, another takes its place.

Stiletto tried to think positive. He reviewed what he knew of the Guardados. How their inside info had crippled cartel efforts in Colombia. The new information Fleming said they promised to hand over once on US soil might cause even more damage. Perhaps, this time, the cartels would suffer lasting effects from whatever the Guardados unleashed. And he'd have a hand in the effort. The results might be more satisfying than simply killing a basement full of expendable street thugs.

He needed to turn his thoughts to optimism instead of brooding and complaining. He laughed to himself. Dr. Gargarin might have said the same thing. Scott decided to bring it up at their next appointment and find out.

The phone on the nightstand rang, a quiet purr which broke his thoughts. He welcomed the distraction and picked up.

"Yes?"

"I hope I didn't wake you," Amaya said.

"No."

"I can't sleep either. Feel like a drink?"

"Why not."

"Give me ten minutes."

"Okay." Stiletto hung up. He left the bed to throw water on his face and rinse with a travel bottle of Scope left on the counter. Beside the bottle was a wrapped toothbrush and sealed toothpaste. The Guardados thought of everything.

Amaya knocked on the door nine minutes later.

———

Sofia Guardado went to the kitchen and asked the cook on duty to fix her something for dinner. She didn't know what her mother was doing but she wasn't in her way so she didn't complain. She ate standing in the kitchen and chased the meal with a bottle of water. Back upstairs in her room, she sat at the vanity and texted Juan again.

S: *You ready to stop being a potato head?*
J: *What do you want now?*
S: *Come get me. I'll meet you on the south road.*
J: *Where's you know who?*
S: *Bitch tits is in a meeting or something. Come get me. I'm leaving now.*
J: *We can't be out long even my dad gets pissed.*
S: *See you in 20 minutes or else.*
J: *Else what?*
S: *Guess!*

She jammed the phone into the back pocket of her jeans and found a jacket in the closet. She left her purse but filled the jacket pockets with odds and ends she might need. She moved two pairs of shoes from a cubby rack and collected a half-full fifth of Jack Daniels. She and Juan had split the bottle on their last outing and she'd wisely saved the second half. It hadn't been easy contraband to acquire. She slipped the bottle into her other jacket pocket.

Now she had to get out and avoid the troops.

Best way?

Through the pool of course!

She opened her bedroom door and stuck out her head. Left, right, all clear. Nobody would stop her moving throughout the house, but she'd rather nobody knew she had left her room at all.

Sofia turned left and walked naturally. It didn't make sense to sneak around and draw attention. She still paused at each corner to see if she was alone, but there was no way to avoid the cameras her parents had placed around the interior. They lurked in the upper corners. After another left, she took stairs down a floor. Let the cameras see her. They'd think she was still inside as long as nobody *outside* saw her.

The wide hallway she stepped into showed her mother's decorating touch rather than her father's. Plants instead of paintings her father preferred lined one side of the hall on marble stands; the opposite side overlooked part of the property. The glass, as usual, was clear and free of dirt and streaks. She walked the length casually. To meet Juan where they had agreed, the south road, Sofia had to slip out via the south side of the house. It was the best way to reach the road, but she had to navigate around a big pool. The pool took up so much space, there was allegedly no way to go around it. You could swim across, of course, but Sofia wasn't wearing a swim suit. There was another way if you watched your step.

Sofia brimmed with nervous energy. She wanted to hurry. The thrill of sneaking out was better than anything Juan might promise once she achieved the goal. Sneaking back in posed its own challenges. Her mother's troops were focused on keeping invaders out, not family members in.

Finally, she reached the end of the hall and faced a

doorway to another balcony. This one overlooked the pool and fancy stone patio. The lights usually on were off. Only small walkway lights glowed around the many pieces of outdoor furniture. She'd have to navigate with care. The patio was above the pool; a curved set of stairs led into the water, which was also dark. If she slipped and fell into the water while skirting the outer edge, all her sneaking around was for nothing, and she'd have a lot of explaining to do. Never mind the consequences of her mother finding the booze in her jacket pocket.

She watched long enough to confirm nobody was patrolling the south side. At the moment anyway.

Down another floor and out onto the dark patio. All the guards must have been checking out the other parts of the ranch. Careful not to bash her foot on a lounger or chair, Sofia angled along the lit walkways to the steps.

She felt flush with heat in the warm air, a combination of the temperature and the adrenaline rushing through her. It was tough not to hurry, but she knew haste would ruin her chances sure as one of the troops shining a spotlight on her.

She looked at the pool. One was supposed to go from the steps to the pool, but if you balanced correctly, you could follow a narrow ledge of stone bordering the pool and jump to the grassy field beyond. Sofia could reach the road by crossing the field; the pool was her primary obstacle.

Sofia paused at the top of the steps. A look back at the hallway windows and balcony above—nobody watching. She faced forward again and listened. No voices, but she caught a whiff of cigarette smoke. She couldn't tell where it came from, or how close it might be. But she also couldn't stand still and wait for more info. Time to go!

Sofia reached the bottom step and followed the thin ledge, leaning over a half wall which supported more of her mother's exotic plants. Leaves brushed her face despite her trying to avoid them.

She cleared the ledge, dropped into a squat and then eased over the side of the lower retraining wall. She stretched one foot out, then the other, and felt the grass. She dropped the rest of the way and stayed low.

The cigarette smell was stronger now and voices carried with the smell.

They were close.

Sofia stayed still and held her breath.

CHAPTER TWENTY

"Nobody's coming in this way," one guard said.

"I suggested land mines in the field once," said the other. "Valdes didn't think it was a viable idea, but he did suggest some other things—"

Only one of the two men smoked, as far as Sofia sensed. The trooper doing all the talking had no time to puff on a butt. Sofia covered her mouth to stifle a laugh as he continued talking. How long did they plan to stand there? They would be near the trees bordering the left side of the field; another tree line was on the right, but beyond those trees was the tennis court.

"This is a lousy route to attack," continued Blabbermouth. "The trees make it a bottleneck. All you need is a few guys on the patio with machine guns and whoever's attacking has nowhere to go."

Sofia wanted to shift her position. Her legs began cramping. Hurry up!

"Come on." More from Blabbermouth as cigarette smoke drifted by. "We gotta cover the front when the guys go on break."

The cigarette smell faded and Sofia tried to stand. Her legs ached. She stayed close to the tree line as she made her way forward once again. She had to lift and plant her feet with care, because she wasn't able to tell how the ground rose and fell in the dark.

Sofia froze midstride as a *pop* broke through the silence; more pops followed, each sound corresponding with the flaring of a light. The line of lights filled the field on the opposite side, and they all shined where she stood.

"Shit!"

Sofia reversed course and ran back toward the house. Alarms joined the lights and she stopped and sucked a mouthful of air when voices reached her ears. Voices of men running in her direction. She caught their moving silhouettes in the shadows of the trees.

She started yelling, "Hey! It's Sofia!"

She held up her hands. The troopers reached her. Sofia's heart dropped into her stomach at the sight of gun muzzles trained in her direction. The one in charge yelled for his men to stand down. She breathed easier when they lowered or slung the weapons.

"What are you doing out here?" the trooper in charge said. He bent over to meet her eyes.

"Get away from me!" she said. "I don't have to tell you anything!" She shoved through the men, snapping, "Don't touch me," as she swatted at them, and they remained behind her as she marched through the trees. She found a path back to the house and the men remained far back. Nobody addressed her.

Until the one in charge said, "It was a nice try, Sofia! We put sensors in the grass for exactly this kind of situation."

"Shut up!" Sofia shouted back.

She burned with another type of heat now. *Embarrassment*. And with the gunners behind her, she couldn't ditch the booze. When they reported her sneaking out to her mother, she'd find the Jack Daniels for sure. Heck, she'd be extra mad because Sofia would have disturbed whatever meeting she was having. And Juan was on his way or waiting for her...

Great. Perfect! I'm such an idiot.

———

Jorge Ramirez thought deeply about his last chat with Valdes. He stood at a window in his own palatial mansion, and appeared as if he waited for the night sky to give him guidance. As leader of the northern branch of the Beltran-Leyva Cartel, the old man was used to making up his mind without taking long.

But this time, he had another's opinion to consider.

He'd updated Fausto Sanchez with their option after Valdes first voiced the need for a strike force, and the other cartel boss had to excuse himself to consult others. After a short deliberation, Sanchez agreed.

Presently, one of his men approached his back. "Jefe." Ramirez turned and took the cordless phone the man offered. Ramirez nodded and the man departed.

"Ramirez speaking."

"It's Sanchez," said the man on the other end of the line. Ramirez felt he and Fausto had forged a tight bond during the project with Valdes.

Which was odd, considering they were normally fierce rivals.

Funny what the chance for billions of dollars does to your outlook.

"Are you ready?"

"I have a detachment of men and helicopters standing by."

"Good. My men and trucks are only waiting for my order as well. But the cost may be high. You do realize we'll take losses."

"It's the reward I'm thinking about Jorge," said Sanchez. "Remember. A Super Cartel. Three points of a triangle we control, because when we're done, I suggest we rid ourselves of Valdes. He's been nothing but bothersome."

"Let's not get too far ahead of ourselves, but, yes, you're not wrong. Who is in charge of your fighting force?"

Sanchez gave him the man's name.

Ramirez said, "My head man will be in touch. They can coordinate. That's all for now."

"May good fortune ride with our people," Sanchez said.

Ramirez grunted. He was too old for hopes and good luck. They'd win by hitting hard and fast and shooting better than the Guardado forces. But he had to acknowledge Sanchez somehow.

"If you say so," he said.

———

Jackeline Guardado examined the half-empty bottle of Jack Daniels and knew better than to use words like "disappointed" with Sofia. The teenager would only grin at the cliché, and stare at her until she left the room.

But she needed the kid to stay put until Stiletto took them out of there.

"You are not to leave this room," Jackeline said

instead, "until I come get you. I will put a guard at the door."

"Fine!"

An escape out the window was a no-go. She was too close to the front porch and the troopers there. Jackeline would tell them to watch anyway.

She let her daughter pout and issued orders to the trooper she'd brought with her, who remained in the hallway beside the door, once Jackeline pulled it closed. She walked back to her office with clenched teeth. Damn kid was going to ruin everything if she wasn't watched.

She met Amaya and Stiletto in the hallway. Before Amaya asked what was wrong, Jackeline unloaded, waiting until they had reached her office and shut the door before concluding the tirade with, "The little brat is too much like me already."

She chucked the Jack Daniels in a desk drawer.

Stiletto said, "Where's Valdes?"

"He's here now," Jackeline told him. "Arrived in the last thirty minutes or so."

"What are you waiting for?"

"I tried to rest like you said, only to have to deal with my child." She put her hands on her hips. "If you want to kill Valdes now, I will call him. He's been trying to see me anyway."

"Where do you want me to wait?"

"East side. We will bring him to you. Got a silencer for your handgun, Mr. Stiletto?"

"I have one, yes."

"I'm surprised you didn't correct me."

"Why? Do I look like I waste time leaving nitpick book reviews on Amazon to show strangers on the Internet what a bad ass I am?"

She smiled.

"One thing I'm curious about," Stiletto said.

"What?"

"My boss told me you have information to bring us. What is it?"

"I was wondering if you'd ask," Jackeline said. She went to a wall safe, punched a combination on the touch pad, waited for a red light to turn green and opened the door. She removed a tablet computer enclosed in a hard case.

"This," she said. "All our secrets."

"Such as?"

"Names of corrupt officials and how much we're paying them and for how long. The names belong to members of the Colombian and United States' governments."

Stiletto felt a chill up his neck.

"I hope there are multiple copies."

"Never fear. The safe is booby trapped. Enter the wrong code, and C-4 in the door will rip off your face and whatever else might be attached. Get past the bomb, you still need to enter a code to unlock the tablet. You have three tries, and then the hard drive fries itself."

"Neither of those are a backup."

"I have everything on the Cloud."

"You've thought this through."

She put the tablet away and closed the safe.

"It can't be a secret whom you pay off," Stiletto said, "unless—"

She faced him. "Go on."

"You're paying somebody who claims to be untouchable, who is quite touchable indeed."

She smiled. "An ace. In the government, yes. You'll love it when I reveal his name."

"You mean *my* government?"

"Maybe both. The impact will be huge."

"Then we're wasting time," Stiletto said. "Let's get Valdes—"

The house shook with a bomb blast. The lights flickered.

Amaya said, "What's going on?"

"It's bad," Jackeline said. She ran to the wall safe and opened the door again. She grabbed the tablet. "My rifle is in my bedroom and I need to get Sofia."

Another bomb blast shook the walls. The three fought to remain standing as a barrage of explosions followed the second, and Amaya shouted, "We're under attack!"

... into the ground again.

CHAPTER TWENTY-ONE

The ground forces of Ramirez and Sanchez moved up the mountain. At the top, through the trees, they overlooked the Guardado ranch. Without the need for orders, ten troopers broke from the main group. The men assembled heavy equipment, hammering bases into the dirt with anchor spikes; when the pieces were completed, five mortar tubes lined the top of the ridge, and the operators zeroed their sights on the ranch.

The force on foot advanced into the valley. They had the strike timed to the second. Mortars first. Ground attack. Then the helicopter gunships Sanchez provided. A second portion of Ramirez troops would roll in via truck to breach the Guardado perimeter. Goals: Kill Jackeline Guardado and link with Manny Valdes to take control of the hacienda.

The mortar crew launched high explosive projectiles at the appointed time, the tubes belching bombs as fast as the operators dropped them down. Bursts of fire and smoke filled the ranch. They were careful not to hit the house. Their orders stated the house should remain intact. The mortars served another purpose. They'd chew up the Guardado foot soldiers and reduce the level of resistance for the ground attack.

The mortar crew ceased fire as the ground force moved through the perimeter. Automatic weapons crackled in the valley non-stop as both sides clashed.

When the helicopters joined the fray, they fired machine guns into the house, and more assault troops rappelled from the choppers to breach the walls and windows and carry the fight inside.

———

The windows shattered, blowing glass inward, as another shockwave rocked the house. Then gunfire started. Stiletto heard choppers approaching.

Jackeline and Amaya shouted at each other in Spanish. Amaya tossed Jackeline her pistol and Jackeline ran out of the room. She clutched the tablet.

"We need more guns than this," Stiletto said, holding up his pistol.

"Follow me to the armory."

"Lead the way!"

Amaya ran out of the office with Stiletto behind her. They had to hurry. Choppers meant troopers were landing on the roof to get into the house. A pistol against multiple assailants with automatic rifles didn't promise success.

"How far?" Stiletto shouted.

"We're close, come on!"

They ran hard.

———

Sofia Guardado screamed as each motor blast made her think the walls would collapse on her. The bedroom windows shattered, cold air, glass, and smoke from outside drifting through the gap. The trooper at her door had rushed in after the first bomb fell, and stood between where the girl lay on the floor, nearly under her bed, and the still-closed door. He held his rifle with one hand, the front portion supported by its sling from around his shoulder. In his left hand, he held a radio, and shouted into the device for help and instructions. Static and garbled yelling came over the speaker in return; none of the noise filled Sofia with much hope. Her mother had to be on the way, though. Sofia knew she wouldn't leave her stuck in the bedroom. But as every agonizing second ticked by, she wondered if the worst had happened, if her mother died on her way to the bedroom. She began to panic.

The trooper stopped shouting into the radio and braced his weapon in both hands. Loud thuds along the hallway made Sofia screech with fright. Somebody was kicking open the doors along the hall and soon—

Boots slammed into her door. The frame splintered as the lock broke. Sofia screamed at the vision of horror in the doorway, a man dressed head-to-toe in black, with a gun as menacing as the violent fire in his eyes.

Sofia's guard fired, blowing the invader into the hallway wall. The man in black fell sideways and hit the floor. A second invader swung the muzzle of his weapon into the bedroom. He and Sofia's guard fired at the same time. The guard fell as bullets chewed through him. He landed a foot from Sofia, and she screamed again. The second invader entered the room, took two steps, and then stiffened as a salvo of slugs hit *him* in the back.

Sofia held her breath as the second invader fell to the

blood-stained carpet. His falling body revealed her mother in the doorway, smoke trickling from the barrel of her pink AK-47.

"Sofia!"

"Mom!"

The girl ran into her mother's arms. Jackeline didn't hug her for long. She ran to the fallen guard to grab his radio.

"Mom, what's happening?"

"Stay away from the door, honey, Amaya's coming."

Jackeline pulled Sofia back from the doorway. She lurched back with her AK at her shoulder as movement in the hall caught her eye. Flame flashed from the muzzle and Jackeline neutralized the threat. The pair of black-clad killers closing on the room fell in a heap, and blocked the hall.

Sofia ran to her mother and grabbed her from behind as Jackeline switched her magazines. She pulled back the bolt. A satchel across her back contained her tablet and spare mags for the rifle.

Chatter over the radio had ceased. She keyed the Talk button.

"Amaya?"

"On the way, stay put if you can," Amaya Olmos responded.

"We're okay for now."

Jackeline tilted her head to look down the hall where the dead men lay. She asked Sofia for a hand-held mirror. Sofia grabbed one from the drawer of her vanity and handed it off with a shaking hand. Jackeline told her to get back. She held the mirror to get a look at the opposite end of the hallway. Clear, for now. The fighting outside remained intense, but at least the bombs had stopped falling.

———

Manny Valdes wasn't ready when the attack began.

And if Ramirez and Sanchez weren't going to alert him ahead of time as promised, did they mean for him to die with the rest of the Guardado crew?

They couldn't kill him as long as he had the tablet they very much wanted, right?

Let's go get the tablet!

He ran from the western section, where he had been checking in with patrols to keep busy, and jumped over a patio wall as the mortars began falling. An explosion rocked the ground as he landed, and knocked him off balance; he fell on his left shoulder. He let out a yell and lost his grip on a pistol. The gun flew from his right hand.

The mortar rounds continued to fall but none touched the house. Bright flashes from the explosions, followed by thick black smoke, filled the property. Valdes coughed as he crawled for his gun. Grasping the pistol once again, he rose. He heard his men—he still thought of them that way—rushing to meet the invaders. Choppers in the distance, getting closer. Their whipping rotor blades sounded louder than normal, but only because Valdes knew who rode in the helicopters. Assault troops who planned to drop onto the roof of the house. The reason the mortar shells didn't touch the building.

Battle sounds filled the night. Guns cracked, men screamed; Valdes knew the Guardado elements were tough, but outnumbered. His "partners" weren't leaving anything to chance. They had every intention of taking the Guardado holdings for themselves, and cutting him out. He was sure.

Rage filled him.

He'd asked for their help, but now they were hanging him out to dry.

His dream of a Super Cartel was on the line, and he wasn't going down without a fight. If he had the precious tablet, he'd have a bargaining chip to stay in the game.

He ran toward the house with an idea of how to intercept *the woman*. If he hurried, he might catch her.

Amaya led Stiletto up a flight of stairs to a hallway. She checked one side, he checked the other; no threats. They moved left and advanced. Amaya kept a US M-4 tight to her shoulder. She and Scott had raided the armory for the M-4s, grenades, Kevlar vests, and other war tools.

She hoped she appeared confident to Stiletto. She didn't feel confident at all. Amaya felt frightened and vulnerable. The Guardados were the only family she had, and somebody wanted to take them away from her.

No.

They moved further along the hall. Her palms sweated on the grip of the M-4. The door to Sofia's bedroom was in sight, and Amaya also spotted two bodies blocking the way ahead. Sporadic shooting echoed from the lower floors. She wished she knew how many had made their way into the house.

"Jackie!"

"In here!"

Amaya and Stiletto quickened their pace. Jackeline and her daughter ran into the hallway to meet them.

Stiletto looked at Jackeline with her pink Kalashnikov and said, "The pink AK isn't a myth."

"I wish it was," Jackeline told him. She dug a spare

from her satchel. "It's ridiculous now. Follow me. I have a car ready to carry us out of here."

"And I have an extraction point," Scott said. He and Amaya kept Sofia between them. Scott gave the girl his Kevlar vest and helped her tie it. They retraced their steps the way they'd arrived.

———

They stopped in an archway to a wider hall with a balcony on one side. Stiletto yelled for the women to get down as men in black crashed through the glass. The helicopters over the roof had deposited the invaders on the balcony, and while the chopper was loud above the crashing glass, it wasn't as loud as Stiletto's M-4 as he engaged. He counted six invaders, the last still in the process of untangling from their rappelling ropes as they rushed inside. The first two dropped as Scott's 5.56mm projectiles ripped through their heads and necks. Scott didn't want to deal with body armor so he aimed high. Sofia screamed; he tuned her out. Jackeline lay flat on the floor in front of him. As he fired over her, she used her Kalashnikov to great effect. Her floor-level bursts kicked the legs out from the invaders not felled by Stiletto's salvos.

Amaya ended the fight. She tossed a grenade. Stiletto covered Jackeline with his body as the grenade detonated, the bang deafening, and the results terrific. Two remaining invaders still standing yelled out in pain as the blasts of shrapnel finished them.

Stiletto rolled off Jackeline and she bounced to her feet, taking the lead again. She fired into the bodies as they passed by. Reaching the end, she checked the way ahead and changed magazines. "Come on!"

Amaya coaxed a petrified Sofia forward. The frightened teen, her face pale, refused to step into the carnage. Stiletto finally scooped her up in his left arm, and carried her above the tangle of bloody arms and legs. He handed her to her mother. Jackeline bent over to look into Sofia's face.

"You can't fall apart, Sofia."

"But, Mom—" Tears filled the girl's eyes.

"Stop it. We're going to your father."

"What?"

"We will explain everything when we're together. You have to stay strong. He's waiting for us."

"Okay." Sofia's voice wavered but Stiletto saw her eyes light up with the news of her Dad. He shouted, "We gotta move, Jackeline."

The cartel queen took the lead again. "Only a little further."

Stiletto hustled to keep up while also watching Amaya and Sofia and their backside. The teen wiped her eyes and kept pace. He hoped her mother's words did the trick. They had an army to fight through before reaching Mike Majors and the extraction point.

CHAPTER TWENTY-TWO

Jackeline led them down a dark hallway and through a set of rooms where Stiletto and Amaya paused to shield Jackeline and Sofia from potential threats. The shooting and fighting continued outside the house; they had found fewer invaders on the way to the garage because the defense from Jackeline's troopers was good, even better than she thought.

They finally reached the garage and Jackeline ran ahead. "Dante?" she called.

Stiletto scanned the garage through the sights of his M-4 carbine. It was hard not to look at all the cars as he completed his sweep. Vehicles were parked two deep on either side, with a wide aisle leading to the exit. Sports and exotics dominated; there were larger SUVs and sedans too. All high-end and expensive. He was looking at millions of dollars in automobiles.

A vehicle across the garage fired to life. A man shouted, "Over here!"

Jackeline and Sofia broke into a run for the Mercedes sedan. Amaya explained to Scott who Dante was as they ran, and Scott followed behind the women. He maintained the danger scan with his focus on the exit. The fighting was louder now, thanks to the thin garage door.

Two gunshots, louder than the rest, echoed; a side door swung open and a man with a pistol entered.

Stiletto shouted, "Get down!"

He fired at Manny Valdes. Valdes ran from the doorway, dove to the floor and crawled to a red Ferrari. Amaya fired on the car; her salvo slammed into the bodywork and struck one of the front tires. The rubber blew and the front end sank.

Stiletto and Amaya alternated bursts of fire as Jackeline and Sofia piled into the Mercedes.

They could shoot the cars all night but if Valdes was pinned, it made sense to get out and deal with Valdes later.

"Go!" Stiletto shouted. Amaya ran to the car. Stiletto fired single shots to cover her. His mag ran dry. He slapped in a reload as he dove into the back of the car.

Amaya had a back window down and her M-4 extended through as they sped along the length of the garage to the exit. She fired blind. Stiletto saw no sign of Valdes and held back. He hoped Amaya's shots kept him down long enough for them to get a head start.

"Hold on!" Dante Costa, behind the wheel, shouted. The garage door was rising but not fast enough for Scott; it looked like they'd hit the bottom edge and damage the roof and windshield.

But the gap widened enough for the Mercedes to plow through. The car fishtailed a little, Dante bringing it back straight as he sped down the drive to the access road.

Stiletto glanced out the back window at the fighting in front of the house. He felt odd. In a way, they were abandoning fellow soldiers; he had to remind himself who he was dealing with for the umpteenth time. He was falling into the trap of thinking these people were normal humans. He pushed the thoughts from his mind and focused on the task in front of him. He could deal with his misplaced quasi-Stockholm Syndrome later. They only thing that mattered was the mission.

He stayed low on the seat and called Mike Majors to advise his fellow Trust operatives he was on the way.

———

Manny Valdes pushed up from the cold floor and ran for the nearest car, a bulletproof Lincoln MKZ. Black in color, it would blend with the night.

He dropped his pistol on the passenger seat and lowered the driver's side visor. The keys slipped from their hiding place and into the palm of his hand.

How hard was it to kill somebody?

Apparently *very* hard, since the Americans became involved.

The engine fired on the first twist of the key. Valdes put the car in gear and left a patch of rubber behind as the tires squealed beneath him.

He still wanted to know *why* the American was there.

And he'd ask before putting a bullet in the man's head.

Valdes steered the Lincoln down the access road, homing on the Mercedes like a heat-seeking missile.

The battle would end here.

Tonight.

———

Amaya spotted the headlights behind them.

"He's behind us!"

Jackeline shouted, "What's he driving?"

"The Lincoln!"

Jackeline cursed. Amaya's face turned red. Stiletto and Sofia looked confused.

"What's the problem?" Stiletto said.

"It's bulletproofed," Jackeline told him.

"Shit," Stiletto said.

"My thoughts exactly," Jackeline said.

———

Stiletto glanced at Sofia. The back of the sedan was large enough for two bench seats, the car having been stretched to accommodate the extra space. The bench seats faced each other; Sofia sat on the floor, knees to her chest, near her mother.

At least she wasn't screaming any longer.

"Where are we going?" Jackeline said.

Stiletto leaned across the forward seat and directed Dante Costa to the extraction point. Costa only nodded; his eyes remained forward.

"He's gaining!" Amaya shouted.

Costa wrenched the wheel and the Mercedes screeched as he made a wide turn onto the main road. He pressed on the accelerator. The engine whined loudly.

"Are the Lincoln's tires bulletproof, too?" Stiletto said.

"Run-flats," Jackeline said.

"This keeps getting better. Shoot the tires when he gets close."

"Why is he going to get close?" Amaya said.

"Because if bullets can't stop the car, he'll use the car to ram us off the road."

"You were right about this getting better," Amaya said.

———

Dante Costa couldn't believe his luck.

He had no doubt what Jackeline carried in her shoulder tote contained the tablet he wanted to get his hands on, and deliver to Ramirez.

All he had to do was find a way to get rid of the white man and Amaya. Jackeline and her AK-47, if he was correct in how she'd react, wouldn't be a problem.

He kept driving, the headlights piercing the darkness ahead, the roadway clear, the slaughter left behind. When the shooting started, he'd hugged the garage floor under the Mercedes. If he couldn't be found, he couldn't be killed by a stray bullet.

Costa glanced in the rearview at his cargo and grinned.

As long as Valdes didn't kill them all, he'd have his chance soon.

CHAPTER TWENTY-THREE

Stiletto plucked a grenade from his web harness. He said to Amaya, "You shoot, I'll toss."

Amaya shoved a fresh magazine into her M-4. "Read my mind."

"Plug your ears, Sofia," Stiletto said.

Stiletto and Amaya powered down the windows on their respective sides. Amaya leaned out with the M-4 and triggered three short bursts. Stiletto pulled the pin on the M26 fragmentation grenade and let the spoon fly. He pitched the grenade out the window, not haphazardly but aiming to keep the explosive on the roadway. If he could blow a hole in the asphalt and cause Valdes to wreck, his bulletproof machine would lose all value.

The Composition B explosive in the M26 detonated with a thunderous crash. The Lincoln swerved, unaffected. The front end grew larger as Valdes pressed the throttle, trying to get closer to reduce the effectiveness of Stiletto's grenades.

Stiletto tossed another, but too quickly. The grenade

skidded across the lanes, off the side of the road, and the blast only kicked up a pile of dirt.

Stiletto held back his last M26. He still had buckshot and smoke charges but neither would be a defense against the big Lincoln. Sparks flashed on the road as Amaya's rounds impacted. Stiletto followed her lead and steadied his M-4 out the window, but before he had a chance to fire, the Lincoln pounded into the Mercedes. The jolt made Stiletto grab for the passenger handle inside the car. The Lincoln backed off a bit, the Mercedes speeding up as Costa gave it more gas. The Lincoln overpowered and collided with the back end a second time. Another crash and jolt. Sofia screamed and pulled her knees closer to her chest. Stiletto held tight but almost fell out the window. He let go of the M-4 and the weapon dangled by its sling, the strap grinding into his neck. He used both hands to pull his body back into the car.

———

If they wanted to get him with bombs, Valdes had a way to mess up their plans.

He stepped on the gas. Not all the way to the floor, but enough for a surge of power. The extra speed took him closer to the back end of the Mercedes sedan. He shifted slightly, aiming for the rear quarter panel. His heavy front end would make a hard impact and if he hit the panel correctly, he'd force the Mercedes to spin out of control. And then everybody inside would be at the mercy of his SIG-Sauer MCX and the .223 slugs within its 30-round magazine.

He pressed the gas pedal a little more.

Closer.

He pounded into the Mercedes once, twice, smiling as he saw the American nearly fall out the window on the right side. But Amaya Olmos held steady, as if planted in the doorway, her weapon wavering ever so slightly. If he looked hard enough, he thought he could stare into her eyes, and what he imagined behind them scared him. She meant to kill him and no mistake. As he started to back off a bit, she fired. Flame flashed from the muzzle of the M-4 and the Lincoln shuddered as the front tire took the blast dead-on. They were run-flats, yes; they were not designed for the near triple-digits speed at which the Lincoln was traveling.

But he had to take the risk.

The front end swayed a little, Valdes correcting with the wheel. Foot on the gas. *Bam!* Into the Mercedes once again. Back off. Surge forward. *Bam!*

And then the sedan's rear end slipped, the car beginning to fishtail as Valdes slammed into the rear quarter one more time. Rubber screeched as the Mercedes spun 360 degrees, across lanes, and off the road. The Lincoln flashed by, Valdes looking in his rearview. A large cloud of dust covered the Mercedes. It did not overturn, or go too far into the trees, and they might make it back onto the road. Valdes slowed the Lincoln and made a U-turn. Time for the *coup de grâce*.

———

Stiletto and Amaya collided with each other as the Mercedes left the road and bounced violently across the rough ground. Costa yelled for everybody to hold on as he fought the spin. The car finally came to a jolting stop mere feet from the trees, and Stiletto began yelling for

Amaya to get out with him and for Jackeline and Sofia to stay inside.

Costa pressed the engine start button, and the motor cranked, but didn't turn over.

Amaya pushed open her door. Jackeline grabbed her by the arm. She turned her back to her friend and boss.

"Make him go away," Jackeline said.

"With pleasure," Amaya told her.

Stiletto and Amaya took cover, Amaya at the bumper and Stiletto at the front end. The engine continued to crank as Costa tried to restart.

Stiletto ignored the Mercedes. His attention was on the straining Lincoln engine, which grew louder by the second. He looked around. Trees behind them. Rocks, boulders, bushes around them. Decent cover but not perfect; the night would help.

The Lincoln screeched to a halt on the road across from the Mercedes.

Amaya opened fire, her rounds bouncing harmlessly off the body of the Lincoln before Valdes exited. But Valdes did exit and roll onto the asphalt, using the bullet-proof vehicle for cover. They couldn't shoot through the car to get him. Stiletto figured either he or Amaya would have to get closer. And that meant leaving their own cover and concealment to get at him.

The gap between them and Valdes didn't look like much, but they'd still be in the open, and all Valdes had to do was not miss.

And if they fell, there'd be nothing to stop Valdes from killing Jackeline and her daughter.

Valdes had all the odds in his favor.

———

Valdes clutched the SIG MCX close to his body. A quick peek under the car allowed him to see Amaya Olmos behind the Mercedes, and the American near the front. Had Jackeline and her daughter left the car for the forest?

No, she'd stay in the car. It was bulletproof and she thought her bodyguard possessed superpowers.

He figured the American was average; he had to not underestimate him, though.

Two shooters to start, then only him and Jackeline.

Amaya stopped firing. He expected the American to shout something, but heard nothing. They were waiting for him to do something.

The idiot behind the wheel stopped trying to restart the car. Finally. Maybe he'd burned out the starter motor. Valdes grinned. Maybe Jackeline was trapped. He had her now for sure. What he needed was a grenade or two.

Why hadn't he brought them?

He had to make a move. Amaya was the biggest threat. Staying flat, he turned and crawled across the grungy asphalt to the rear of the Lincoln. He'd have a better shot at Amaya. Hell, maybe the American would give up once he realized Valdes was the better of them.

Only one way to find out.

———

Stiletto spotted movement between the ground and the bottom of the Lincoln but not enough for a shot. He had another idea, though.

He took inventory of his leftover grenades. The night's darkness didn't make it easy so he felt each one as it hung on his chest rig. One last M26 high explosive, one smoke, one buckshot.

He put a plan together. He'd have to carry it out without signaling Amaya; in fact, he needed her to keep Valdes busy.

Valdes finally opened fire. His rounds smacked the Mercedes, bouncing off the bulletproof glass, slicing through the outer metal to smack the armor plating beneath. He was firing for effect, trying to scare him and Amaya into responding. Amaya fired back. Valdes shifted his aim and shot at her. *Now!* Stiletto plucked the smoke grenade from his harness, pulled the pin, and pitched.

The grenade arced high before dropping solidly on the ground between the Lincoln and the Mercedes. The grenade popped, thick smoke billowing from either end. The hiss overpowered the gunfire, and soon the shooting stopped as neither Amaya or Valdes had anything resembling a target any longer.

The lack of wind kept the smoke cloud centered between the cars and Stiletto took every advantage. He left the car and circled around the edge of the cloud to drop flat, in line with the Lincoln. Better, he was lined up with Valdes's prone form too.

The wannabe cartel kingpin must have sensed the movement, because he rolled onto his back, brought around the muzzle of his weapon, and let a burst go as Stiletto rolled to avoid the salvo. The shots zipped by, whistling as they sliced through the air, and Stiletto answered with his compact carbine, the M-4 bucking against his shoulder as the three-round burst left the muzzle.

The bullets struck Valdes's body with wet slaps, punching through flesh and tumbling end-over-end as they plowed through bones and organs. Valdes screamed, his body tightening up and the rifle falling from his grasp.

Stiletto rose to a knee, keeping his sights on Valdes.

"I got him, Amaya!"

Before the words left his mouth, Amaya Olmos ran to him. Stiletto arrived to find him still alive, his eyes locked on Scott's in defiance, but his breathing ragged and coming only in sharp gasps.

Amaya shouldered her rifle. "Hey."

Valdes ignored her. He stayed focused on Scott.

"Finish him," Stiletto said.

Amaya walked around Valdes to stand beside Scott. Scott stepped back. Valdes finally looked at her. His mouth twisted into a snarl. She fired single shots, the weapon popping repeatedly, spent brass tinkling on the pavement, until nothing remained of Valdes's face except churned, bloody flesh. The ground beneath him turned into a red-brown mud.

Amaya slapped a fresh mag into the M-4. Stiletto noticed it was her last.

"Come on," Stiletto said. "Let's see if we can get the Mercedes moving."

"Right."

They walked toward the Mercedes waving leftover smoke out of their way.

CHAPTER TWENTY-FOUR

As the smoke began to clear, Dante Costa finally recognized his opportunity. But it meant nothing if he couldn't get the car started.

Jackeline Guardado wasn't watching him. Her attention was out a back window, watching the battle, one hand on her ridiculous pink AK-47 and another keeping her daughter from seeing what was happening outside. Sofia was on the floor, her wide eyes locked on her mother for information or reassurance or both.

Costa looked at the starter button. He *needed* the car to start. So far, it hadn't.

Two figures moving through the fading smoke forced him into action. Costa pressed the starter button again. The engine cranked and strained to start. The figures did not hurry. The American and Amaya had no reason to think he was about to take off with Jackeline, her kid, and, most importantly, the tablet computer in her shoulder bag.

He let off the button and counted to five. The American and Amaya were close enough to make eye contact through the glass. He thought Amaya was staring at him. *No. It's all in your head.*

Costa hit the start again. The engine finally turned over with a burble from the exhaust pipe. Jackeline's daughter gasped and shouted, "We can go!" and then Costa shifted into drive and stepped on the gas. The Mercedes kicked up a geyser of dirt and surged forward. Costa aimed the car at the American and Amaya. The American pulled her out of the way. The pair tumbled to the ground in a clumsy roll. Costa steered for the road. The tires chirped as they bit into the pavement, and then they were speeding away.

Now he had to deal with Jackeline. She turned her startled expression his way. They made eye contact in the rearview mirror. As the car traveled further from the scene of the gunfight, she didn't speak. She told Sofia to move out of her way and turned her AK on the back of Costa's head.

The rifle was too big to maneuver in the cabin, but she managed to get the muzzle through the gap between back and front and touched Costa's neck.

"What are you doing?"

"You kill me, we'll crash."

"We've crashed already. Answer me!"

"If I die and the car rolls, the armor might not save you, Mrs. Guardado."

"Tell me what's happening!"

Costa didn't answer. He stepped hard on the brakes. The car's nose pitched forward; Sofia let out a scream; Jackeline flew forward too. The muzzle of her rifle jabbed deeper into Costa's neck, but only for a second. He shifted and momentum carried her forward. She crashed into the backrest of the reversed rear seat, her rifle protruding into the front. Costa grabbed her gun.

With his seatbelt fastened, he had to shift awkwardly, crying out under the sudden muscle strain as he wrenched the AK out of Jackeline's grip. The rifle was too long to come all the way through, but he managed to slam the buttstock into Jackeline's face.

The buttstock struck hard and split her skin. Jackeline recoiled, hands over her face, Sofia yelling. Costa pulled the AK the rest of the way through the gap and set it on the passenger seat. Sofia fussed with her mother; Costa heard crying; he ignored all as he stepped on the gas again and resumed driving.

He had a delivery to make.

"What the hell is he doing?" Amaya shouted. She lay beneath Stiletto, who'd grabbed her as the Mercedes barreled toward them and flung them both to the ground. They rolled away from the car and now watched the receding tail lights with stunned expressions.

"Who was he?" Stiletto asked.

"My sorta boyfriend."

"Can you reach him?"

"If my phone isn't destroyed, sure."

Scott helped her up. Both coughed. The smoke from the grenade was mostly gone, but some lingered.

"Do I call him now?"

Stiletto said, "I have a feeling your boyfriend was working for Valdes, or at least the same people Valdes was working for. I don't think he panicked and will be coming back for us."

"Jackeline has her gun—"

"And her kid. I'm sorry, Amaya, if she hesitates, your boyfriend has the edge."

"His name is Dante."

"You get to kill him then."

"I appreciate it, but it's cart before horse at this point."

"I have my people close by." Stiletto suggested they hide in the tree line in case Valdes had any friends on the way. She agreed. Concealed from the road, Stiletto reached out to Mike Majors with the update. A confused Majors asked questions Stiletto had no answer for; all he could do was repeat what had happened. Scott emphasized they needed to link up and plan their next move, because as far as he was concerned, the rival cartels, or at least one of them, now had open access to Jackeline, her daughter, and whatever secrets she carried on the tablet computer.

Majors said, "We've come too far to lose now."

"I agree," Scott said. "We are on the way. Let the General know. We might need some help too."

"There's no time to wait. It's us or nobody."

Stiletto wasn't going to argue over the phone. He told Majors to expect him and Amaya soon.

———————

Majors ended the call with a curse. He yelled for Ellis and McCoy and the two agents ran to him. Majors explained the situation. They had Scott and Guardado's bodyguard coming, but no Jackeline or Sofia.

"Any idea where they're being taken?" Ellis asked.

"None," Majors said. "Worse, I have no idea how we're going to get her back with five shooters and limited ammo."

McCoy added, "Scott is probably running low on ammo too."

"All right," Majors said, "here's what we do. I'll keep watch and you two break out the spare bullets. We'll see what we can do for them when they get here."

Ellis and McCoy departed for the truck and extra supplies, while Majors resumed his post and waited for Stiletto's arrival.

CHAPTER TWENTY-FIVE

The indicator on Majors' right wrist began flashing. He radioed to Ellis and McCoy that Stiletto and Amaya were inside the electronic perimeter.

He clicked off the safety on his rifle. He wouldn't know for sure it was Scott and the woman until they were close enough to identify, and in the dark, recognition meant a verbal password. If whoever appeared gave the wrong answer, Majors planned to put the HK416 carbine into action and let a salvo of 5.56mm slugs do the talking.

Ten minutes went by. The chill of the night didn't affect him. His combat fatigues kept him warm, and the surge of adrenaline running through him kept up his pulse rate. He'd relax when Stiletto showed up. The crickets, disturbed by the motion in the forest, had stopped chirping. Eventually he heard footsteps, and when a shadowy figure finally appeared ahead, he took aim.

"Flash," he said. The code wasn't hard. Stiletto only needed to provide a one-word answer.

"Thunder," Scott said.

Majors let out a breath and rose from his position. He motioned Stiletto forward. Another figure, thinner than Scott, stepped from her own cover and followed him into the camp.

"Hello," Stiletto said.

"This wasn't what I expected," Majors said.

"Same. Mike, this is Amaya Olmos, Jackeline Guardado's bodyguard." Majors shook her hand and Stiletto introduced her to Ellis and McCoy as well. The pair said they had enough ammo to refill a couple of their spent magazines, and while Stiletto and Amaya reloaded the empty magazines while sitting on the tail gate of Majors' Land Rover, they discussed the situation. McCoy cracked a couple of blue chemical lights so they had some illumination instead of facing each other in the darkness.

Majors listened quietly as they repeated most of the information Stiletto had given over the phone, but then Amaya took over, explaining her relationship with Dante Costa.

"Has he ever," Majors said, "shown any disloyalty to the Guardados before?"

"No," she said. "I can't explain this at all. I figured he'd panicked, and would stop and come back, but we gave him enough time, don't you think, Scott?"

"Long enough."

"So, yeah, he's taken Jackeline and Sofia. He has some kind of other agenda. What it might be, I have no idea."

"But you can call him?" Majors said.

Amaya unzipped her combat vest far enough to reach into an inside pocket. She pulled out her cell phone, and turned it over a few times in the glow of the blue light. "Not broken," she announced. She selected Dante

Costa's name from her contact list and switched the phone to speaker mode. Stiletto scooted closer to her to hear.

The line clicked. Costa spoke loudly, sounded stressed.

"What is it, Amaya?"

"Bring her back right now."

Costa laughed. "Let me tell you the score, sweetie. Jorge Ramirez wants Mrs. Guardado's tablet, and everything else. I'm going to deliver."

"Was it Ramirez who attacked the hacienda?"

"I suppose. They didn't tell me," Costa said.

"Bring her back and we'll double whatever Ramirez is paying."

Costa laughed again. "You can't afford me. My reward will be bigger than any amount you can imagine, Amaya. Not even your ass is enough."

Stiletto thought he saw her turn red in the blue light.

"I'm going to kill you, Dante," Amaya said. "I'm going to stick a gun in your mouth and blow the back of your neck out."

"You have to find me first."

Another voice in the background came over the speaker. A woman. Jackeline. Shouting.

"Amaya, you know what to do!"

The line clicked as Costa ended the call. Amaya, very calmly, returned the cell to her vest. She scooted off the tail gate and walked a few steps, stopped, and kept her back to the men. Stiletto held up a hand when Majors started toward her. Majors stopped.

Stiletto figured Majors wanted to know the same thing he did. What was Amaya supposed to do? Was there a plan in place for such an emergency as this?

Amaya remained quiet. She didn't address the men.

Stiletto watched her. After a few minutes, he said, "Amaya?"

"We need to go and get her," Amaya said. She turned around and returned to the tail gate. "I know where Jorge Ramirez sleeps. He's easy to find, and he'll keep Jackeline—"

"Whoa," Majors said.

"Yes, back up," Stiletto added. "We have a serious problem. There's only five of us, and as you can see, we are low on ammo and supplies."

"I can get us all the guns and ammo we need," she said.

"Can you get us another thirty shooters?" Majors asked.

"I can get us sixty shooters, or more, depending on who might be available."

"And who are we going to ask?" Stiletto said.

"It's a group called *El Tigre*. Anti-cartel commandos. *Sicarios* hand-picked from the police and military and sorted into quick-strike units."

"Never heard of 'em, Amaya," Stiletto said.

"But you've seen their work," she added.

"You said *anti*-cartel. They might agree to hit Ramirez, but help Jackeline?" Stiletto raised an eyebrow. "Do you have something on the leader?"

"*El Tigre* is led by Victor Ramos."

Stiletto blinked.

Majors said, "Holy shit."

"The mercenary?" Stiletto said.

"The same. The butcher of Central America. Or the hero. Depends on who's dead."

"What's the connection with Jackeline?" Stiletto said. "I still don't understand how going to him will help us."

"Victor came before Carlos."

"I see," Stiletto said. "He still has a soft spot for Jackeline?"

"She thinks so. It's worth a risk. He's never moved against the Guardado Cartel; in fact, Carlos gave him information several times over the years. He might even know the family secret."

"Uh-huh," Stiletto said. "Where do we find this guy?"

"He's not hard to find. Maybe a day's hike."

Stiletto glanced at Majors. "What do you think?"

"Doesn't matter what I think," Majors said. "If she says he'll help, we need to talk to him. We also need to let General Ike know what's going on."

Stiletto sighed. "Yeah. I'll call him. He'll be wondering why I didn't get in touch earlier."

"Secure phone up front in the truck if you want," Majors said.

Stiletto left the tail gate and climbed behind the wheel. The secure phone sat in the center console. He picked up the unit and dialed headquarters.

CHAPTER TWENTY-SIX

The Mercedes turned onto a dirt road. The suspension worked to soften the bumps, but the speed at which Costa drove made Jackeline and Sofia rock and bump into each other as they sat on the floor.

Jackeline pressed a hand to the cut on her face and held back any reaction. She didn't want Sofia to see or hear her in pain. Sofia pulled at her hand—"Let me see it, Mom,"—and Jackeline relented. She didn't know what Sofia expected to see, but the girl said, "It doesn't look bad," and then pulled her T-shirt out of the waistband of her jeans. Sofia tore a strip from the bottom of the shirt and folded it into a square. She put it in her mother's hand and her mother pressed the cloth to the wound. Jackeline wasn't sure it made any difference, but she was happy to see her kid trying.

But this situation was what she had wanted to spare her child from. Instead, Sofia was in the thick of the violence, and a fifteen-year-old didn't have the knowledge or experience to handle the situation.

How would Sofia deal with the aftermath?

Assuming they survived.

It was the future Jackeline was thinking of as the car continued to buck.

"Slow down!" she shouted. Costa glanced back at her in the rearview. He did slow the car, though. Jackeline sat up. She looked through the gap between the front and back and attempted to discern where they were. The headlamps only highlighted portions of trees on either side of the road. She leaned back again.

Sofia snuggled close. Jackeline held her with her left arm.

"Not much further," Costa announced.

"I'm going to kill you, Dante," Jackeline announced.

Costa laughed.

Both women uttered startled cries as the Mercedes hit a big bump.

———

Costa slowed the Mercedes some more. He'd burned through half the gas tank, the needle pointing at the center position, and he was glad he'd filled up before departing. If he hadn't, they'd have faced a bigger challenge. And he didn't need any more challenges.

He scanned the right side of the road looking for a gap in the trees. There was no sign announcing the turn; you had to know it was there. He slowed to ten miles an hour and creeped along. When the gap appeared, he turned the wheel. Finally, the car was back on concrete. Costa still kept the speed down, as he was now on the access road to Jorge Ramirez's estate.

In the back, Jackeline nudged Sofia. The girl moved away from her mother. Jackeline sat up again to peer out. A sense of dread came over her. She recognized the steel barriers on either side of the road which kept over-growth from encroaching on the pavement.

"Where are we?" Sofia whispered.

Jackeline pulled Sofia close again. "Don't worry."

But she was worried. She removed the torn cloth from her face and felt to see if the wound was still bleeding. The pressure she'd applied appeared to have worked. The bleeding had stopped. She pressed the cloth to her skin again to make sure.

Now it made sense. Valdes had made a deal with Jorge Ramirez to take over her organization. But why bring her to the estate? The answer dawned slowly, and Jackeline looked at her shoulder bag on the floor of the car. Ramirez wanted her tablet computer and the data contained within the hard drive. He wanted the operational details and the names of those she'd bribed to let the drug business flourish.

The tablet gave her a chance. Ramirez couldn't kill her until she gave up the code to unlock the contents. But a chill ran up her back. Ramirez would use Sofia to get her to crack.

Oh, Carlos, what have we done?

She let go of the cloth and wrapped Sofia in both arms, clutching her tightly.

They won't harm my daughter. Whatever it takes we're getting through this in one piece.

The Mercedes made another right turn, continued for a short stretch, then slowed and stopped.

Costa set the parking brake.

———

Jorge Ramirez and three of his shooters walked down the porch steps to the edge of the access road where the

Mercedes sat. The door opened and Dante Costa stepped out.

"Do you have them?" Ramirez said.

"In the back." Costa moved quickly to the rear door. He opened the back, and the overhead lamp spotlighted Jackeline and Sofia on the floor.

"Mrs. Guardado, this is a pleasure. I'm sorry to see the trip wasn't as pleasant as it should have been."

She stared at him. Ramirez recognized the stare of a woman capable of violence, as he knew she very well was. In her youth, anyway. Did she still have the power? The girl watched Ramirez out of the corner of one eye. The child would be Jackeline's Achilles heel, but even then, Ramirez knew, he'd have to tread with care.

"Are you going to step out under your own power, or do my men need to drag you out?"

Jackeline snapped, "Keep them back, Jorge."

"Very well. The night is warm. Step out of the car, Mrs. Guardado."

Jackeline nudged her daughter. Sofia pulled clear and scooted to the rear seat. Jackeline exited first, brushed off her clothes, and reached back for Sofia. The girl refused to move. Jackeline spoke reassuringly, and eventually Sofia agreed. She joined her mother outside the car, but stayed partially behind her.

Ramirez snapped orders to two of his shooters. "Take them to Building C. Do not harm them."

The two shooters, with their menacing submachine guns pointing at the women, grabbed them and shoved them ahead. Jackeline and Sofia started walking with the gunners close behind. They started up a rise toward a small building twenty yards from the main house.

Ramirez smiled at Costa.

"And the computer?"

"Inside still."

Ramirez raised an eyebrow. Costa took the hint and reached into the Mercedes, grabbed the shoulder bag, and handed it to Ramirez.

The older cartel baron held the bag and felt the weight within, but it didn't mean the computer was there. He unbuttoned the flap and looked inside, pulled out the tablet, and nodded. At least it was a tablet computer. Whether it was *the* tablet he still had to figure out.

"Good work, Dante."

"Thank you, Mr. Ramirez."

Ramirez turned to the third shooter.

"Take him away and kill him."

The third shooter grabbed Costa with force, twisting an arm behind his back as he struggled and shouted in protest. Ramirez ignored the pleas. The shooter raised his weapon to hammer Costa in the back of the head, but not with such force to knock him unconscious. The blow took the fight out of Costa, however, and he staggered a little as the pair continued back along the access road. They were on the east side of the property, and a small creek cut through the land on that side. Ramirez had left many a body in the creek water.

He took a deep breath and turned to go back into the house. He had to secure the tablet before addressing Jackeline and her daughter again.

———

The shooters escorting Jackeline and Sofia into Building C shoved them through the doorway. Sofia stayed on her feet but Jackeline stumbled, falling to her hands and knees. Sofia rushed to her side. Jackeline brushed her off and rose again.

Overhead light snapped on. Jackeline looked around. At least it wasn't a concrete cell, or an underground dungeon, which she certainly had expected. Instead, the interior looked like a storage room with sealed boxes and miscellaneous loose items, none of which looked like weapons. She might find a useful item, but she needed time to sort.

One of the shooters slung his submachine gun and dug two folding chairs from behind a stack of items in a corner. He set the chairs in the center of the room and gestured for the woman to sit. Jackeline nudged Sofia again and the girl complied. Jackeline took the other chair. She crossed her legs and sat with an air of control she didn't feel. She had to maintain a strong front for both her and her daughter.

The shooters didn't close the door. They stood to either side, casually holding their weapons. Insects buzzed in and out. Sofia waved a fly away.

When Ramirez returned, his bulk filled the doorway a moment. His face looked hard, his lips a flat line.

"You know what I want," he said.

"Go to hell, Jorge."

"I might. But you're going to give me the codes to your computer before I go."

Jackeline grunted. She folded her arms.

"I'm going to tell my men not to lay a hand on you," Ramirez said, "unless they desire to be fed to my alligators. You know of my pets, don't you?"

She did. She said so.

"I could easily tell them to hang you from the ceiling by your wrists, then beat and rape you repeatedly. And your daughter too. But I'm not a barbarian.

I'm also not unreasonable. Cooperate with me, and you might live."

Jackeline scoffed. "What else do you have in your repertoire, Jorge? Come on, now. Get on with it."

Ramirez turned to his men. "Take the daughter."

The gunners moved forward and grabbed Sofia. She screamed and tried to fight but the powerful men held her in control. Jackeline jumped from the chair with a balled fist, but never landed a blow. One of the shooters punched her in the stomach and she doubled over, collapsing, Sofia screaming with streaming tears as the pair hauled her out. Jackeline struggled to breathe as she started to get up, Sofia's cries echoing in her mind.

A hand grabbed a fistful of her hair. Ramirez tugged and threw her onto her back. He stood over her. She scooted back but his imposing frame towered over her.

"You're going to regret this, Mrs. Guardado."

Jackeline, flush with heat, managed to get out a reply. "I'll murder you myself, Jorge."

"We'll see."

Ramirez left the room and shut the door. Jackeline stayed on the floor until she could breathe again. Her belly hurt. Her heart hurt. She ran to the door and turned the knob, but it didn't budge. They'd locked her in the room and her daughter was alone out there. She pounded on the door as she screamed.

———

Ramirez returned to his second-floor office where his number two, Harry Donaldo, waited.

"Did you get it?"

Ramirez held up the shoulder bag. He placed the bag on his desk.

"She's going to be difficult," the cartel leader announced.

"Did we expect anything less?"

Ramirez ignored the question and picked up the desk phone. He dialed Fausto Sanchez and waited for the connection.

"Yes," his partner said.

"It's me," Ramirez said. "We have Jackeline and her kid. And the computer."

"Good."

"What's happening at the house?"

"Our people have subdued the resistance and are now searching the house for anything useful."

"Keep me posted. I'm going to work on the women and get Jackeline to crack. We need her access code to the computer. I have a feeling it won't be easy."

"There are ways."

"I'm aware there are ways, Fausto." Ramirez hung up and turned to Donaldo. "I told two of the troops to remove the girl from her mother's presence. Go make sure she is unmolested. I will not go to extreme measures until there is no other way."

"*Si, jefe,*" Donaldo said. He went out.

Ramirez checked his watch. It was quite late. He wanted to sleep. Keeping Jackeline up all night worried about her kid might soften her up to the point where she'd agree to his requests.

If not, he'd unleash hell.

CHAPTER TWENTY-SEVEN

Stiletto finished updating General Ike and hooked the satellite phone with a grunt of frustration. He wasn't upset about his orders to continue the mission; he didn't need the order, they were going to get Jackeline and Sofia back, orders or not. He was frustrated with what should have been a clean job going off the rails, and dangerously so. He didn't think about his previous misgivings; they were irrelevant now.

He left the truck and returned to Majors, Amaya, Ellis, and McCoy.

"Fleming is on board with whatever we do," Stiletto said. "But he also recommends we get some rest."

"Moving about at night looking for *El Tigre*," Amaya said, "isn't a good idea. I agree."

"We ain't the Hilton," Majors said. "Amaya, why don't you sleep in the back of the truck. We'll stay out here."

Amaya had no problem with the arrangement. She had seen worse.

Stiletto woke her in the morning with a tug on an ankle. She wiped her eyes and joined the men for breakfast, which wasn't any more glamorous than the sleeping conditions. Cold rations, warmed over a fire, at least filled their bellies, and the instant coffee included in the MRE packs washed it all down.

Packing up the camp took less than an hour. Majors collected the electronic sensors from where he'd placed them, and they loaded everything into the Rover. Majors drove while Amaya sat in the passenger seat to direct him. Stiletto was jammed in back with Ellis and McCoy. Their weapons and web harnesses made the limited space more cramped.

Amaya's directions led them deep into the jungle, over rough terrain, and Majors had to go slow over the natural obstacles. Luckily no fallen trees blocked their path; the jungle road appeared well-traveled, with overgrowth kept to a minimum via a constant stream of vehicles going through.

An hour of slow travel went by.

"We're almost there," Amaya said.

"How will we know?" Majors asked.

And then the dot of a laser sight landed on his chest.

"Stop the truck," Amaya said.

Majors threw the car into park as a man began shouting for them to get out of the Rover. Majors didn't move. "Should I?"

"Do it," Amaya said as she opened her door.

The crew left the Rover. Stiletto told everybody to stay cool as men in camouflage, their faces painted with green streaks, emerged from concealment. Stiletto turned back and forth to take in the scene. At least fifteen gunners surrounded them, some in the branches of trees. The sniper who'd put the laser dot on Majors' chest was perched on a branch ten yards ahead. The snout of his rifle covered them.

Amaya responded to the orders with her own string of rapid Spanish, and the leader of the group approached her. His finger rested on the trigger of his Kalashnikov.

Stiletto examined the man. He appeared bulky beneath his uniform and combat harness. Dark hair extended below his combat cap. Whatever Amaya said at least made him willing to talk, and they had a short exchange.

She turned to them. "They'll escort us to the camp. It's about one hundred yards from here."

Stiletto checked out the cold eyes of the gunners near him. None of them seemed to have relaxed despite the leader's conversation with Amaya.

"I'm not sure about this, Amaya."

"I know. But please trust me. What sense does it make for me to lead us into a trap?"

"It doesn't."

"Then let's get back in the Rover and follow."

More slow driving, with the foot soldiers spread out in a phalanx to escort them through. The team leader and the sniper from the tree remained up front in the roadway.

Stiletto took a deep breath and willed himself to calm down. This wasn't his first exposure to anti-cartel vigilantes, but it was his first time being up close and personal. Such commando groups as *El Tigre* had formed throughout Colombia in response to the government's failure to prevent cartel violence. The vigilante group were victims of the cartels. They'd lost friends, family members, children; they'd been personally affected, somehow, and wanted revenge. Stiletto understood. He appreciated the groups ignored repeated calls from the government to disarm and disband, but he also knew if they suspected foul play from Amaya and his team, they'd be shot without a second thought. Success or failure of the mission depended on convincing *El Tigre*'s leader of their intentions.

The question of whether they'd help once they learned Jackeline Guardado was involved remained the biggest concern on Stiletto's mind. Despite what Amaya described as his previous relationship with her, he wasn't certain they'd find support among the force.

They entered the camp. They'd cleared a portion of the jungle to set up Quonset huts and tents. More men, and women, in camouflage watched the Rover enter. Then the leader and sniper gestured for them to exit. They stepped out of the Rover again, and the patrol approached aggressively. The leader demanded they turn over their weapons, and Amaya and the Americans did so. Stiletto's unease grew. If the vigilantes decided not to help, they'd have a hell of a time evading the bullets sure to come their way.

The patrol leader snapped an order. Amaya translated. They were to follow him and did so, through the camp, to a large tent with an open front. Within the tent stood several camouflaged men, one taller than the others, along with computers, maps pinned to walls, and a set of tables pushed together.

"The tall one is Ramos," Amaya said.

Stiletto and the other Trust agents remained quiet.

The patrol leader told them to stop. He approached Ramos and began talking; Ramos asked Amaya for more information, which she supplied. The conversation took three minutes by Stiletto's count, and Ramos's eyes roamed over them carefully. Scott hoped he detected they were honest souls and not vipers attempting to sneak into the camp. He had a feeling if they hadn't had Amaya with them, they'd have already been shot.

Amaya spoke some more, and Ramos turned his attention to her. He asked a few questions, and she answered each. Finally, he nodded.

Amaya turned to them. "All right, we can at least talk about the situation. No promises."

"Do we get our guns back?" Majors asked.

"No," she said.

Ramos spoke again. Amaya looked at Scott and translated.

"He wants to see you alone first, Scott."

Stiletto nodded. "All right."

———

The patrol leader, with his Kalashnikov, stayed close. Victor Ramos, the butcher of Central America, led Stiletto a few feet away from the tent. Scott ignored the other activity around him. His current world focused on the leader of *El Tigre*.

"What is your name?" Ramos said, in perfect English.

"Scott Stiletto. I'm an American agent, as are my men."

"Amaya told me a tall tale."

"I can't tell you everything, but Jackeline Guardado is very important to my people back home."

"I think I know why."

"Do you?"

"You're aware of our previous relationship?"

"Amaya mentioned it."

"I would have married that woman," Ramos said, "had certain events not transpired."

"I understand." Scott didn't want to pry, but he had an idea tragedy had struck Ramos directly, sparking his hatred toward the cartels. Why else would he assemble a vigilante commando group?

"She has helped my people before," Ramos said. "I've put two-and-two together, as you Americans say, and have a few thoughts on why."

"You should go with those thoughts."

"What do you mean?"

"I mean you're probably correct."

"And now you need her? Do you already have Carlos?"

"I can't confirm anything, sir."

Ramos sighed. "We deal in suggestions, suppositions, and assumptions."

"Sure."

"I prefer the direct approach."

"As do I," Stiletto said, "but in this case, I have people to protect."

"Jackeline and her daughter."

"Yes, sir."

"Your think Ramirez has them?"

"The conversation with Amaya's boyfriend leads us to believe that, yes."

"Ramirez won't harm them right away," Ramos said. "We have time, but not much."

"Does this mean you'll help us?"

"I was a father once," Ramos said. "She was killed in a cartel gun battle. Caught in a crossfire. Her mother died too. When I buried them, I buried myself as well. I now exist only to give the cartels ten times what they inflicted on me."

"I have a child myself," Stiletto said. "I get it."

"She's young still?"

"An adult now, but you know—we always see them as babies."

"It's not easy being a father."

"It is not, sir. Indeed, it is not."

"Take care of her."

Stiletto nodded. He added nothing more.

"I could never hurt Jackeline," Ramos continued. "To see her in danger, and Sofia. No. I must do something."

"It's going to cost."

"I've already lost everything," Ramos said. "As have many of my people. We're all here for the same reason. The war gives us life. I don't expect you to understand."

"I understand more than you think."

"Yes, we will help. I've wanted to attack Ramirez a long time, but circumstances keep interfering. We will accept the distractions no more."

"We are in your debt," Stiletto said. "I can't make any promises—"

"I require nothing from the United States. This is a personal struggle."

"We will show our gratitude, sir. I can promise that much."

Ramos suggested they go back to his tent. Stiletto followed. The patrol leader, with his hot eyes and ever-ready weapon, followed.

———

Victor Ramos rolled a large paper map across one of the tables. Stiletto examined the details.

"This is where Ramirez lives," Ramos said. He stood on the opposite side from Scott. Amaya remained off to the side, watching but otherwise uninterested. Majors, Ellis, and McCoy looked over the map with Scott.

The Ramirez spread was significant. Ramos explained it covered forty acres. A golf course ringed the estate on three sides; the fourth side, on the east end of the property, contained a parking area and an adjacent creek.

"It is well-guarded," Ramos said. "Our biggest problem is a rumored escape tunnel under the main house, here." He pointed to the main house at the center of the property. "We'd need to get him before he can get to the tunnel."

"You've never confirmed the tunnel is really there?"

Ramos shook his head. His gaze remained on the map.

"If you can get us in there," Stiletto said, "you can have Ramirez. We only want Jackeline and Sofia."

Ramos nodded. Then he lifted his head from the map to look at Scott.

"There are other rumors," the vigilante leader said.

"Such as?"

"Ramirez has a close relationship with Fausto Sanchez, who belongs to another cartel."

"The Plancarte Cartel," Amaya chimed in.

"It has been suggested," Ramos said, "there are Guardado elements also sharing in the association."

"Valdes," Amaya said again.

Ramos looked at her with a raised eyebrow. Amaya quickly explained, adding: "Valdes is dead. We killed him. He can't tell us anything."

"What about—"

"I can only assume," she said, "Dante Costa was also involved."

"Ramirez would have shot him by now," Ramos said. "He'll be no help in clearing this up."

Stiletto said, "If they were working together, what was the goal?"

"Combining three cartels into one," Ramos said. "It

explains why they want Jackeline. Why they haven't killed her. She has something they need still."

The tablet, Stiletto thought. He added nothing to Ramos's statement.

But Ramos already knew. "Jackeline has information on who she's bribed, and other details related to what she and her husband did. Ramirez and Sanchez will need that data to maintain continuity. If the payments to officials stop, the protection ends. They can't risk losing those resources while they consolidate."

"Makes sense," Stiletto said.

Ramos looked down at the map again and nodded. "I have men and choppers. We can be ready in three hours."

"We are at your disposal, sir," Stiletto added.

"Let's go get Jackeline," Ramos said.

CHAPTER TWENTY-EIGHT

Jackeline lay on the floor, curled in a corner, trying to use her right arm for a pillow. She slept poorly. And why wouldn't she? Sofia wasn't with her, and may have been subjected to a terrible ordeal overnight. The only consolation Jackeline felt was she hadn't heard any screaming. But it didn't mean much. They may have taken her far enough away from Building C so Jackeline couldn't hear.

Footsteps shuffled outside the door. The lock clicked, the door swung open, and Sofia yelped as she was pushed inside. The door slammed and locked again.

"Sofia!" Jackeline sprang from the floor, going to her daughter, who remained where she'd fallen. Jackeline grabbed her, holding her close as she ran a hand over her to check for wounds. She examined the girl's clothes. None had been disturbed. Sofia sobbed into Jackeline's chest. They hadn't hurt her other than keeping her away from her mother. Ramirez was good at head games. Mental torture. Relief flooded over Jackeline anyway as she rocked her daughter gently and tried to assure her everything would be okay. She wasn't sure she believed her own words.

Amaya, you know what to do!

It was the only thing Jackeline could hold onto. The only thing giving her hope. How long would it take for her and the Americans to reach *El Tigre*? Would Victor agree to help? He had to. He *had* to.

In the meantime, Jackeline had to reach deep down and remember who she once was. The deadly *sicaria*. The sharpshooter who used more than a rifle to kill her enemies.

She had to for Sofia's sake.

"Sofia," she said into her daughter's ear.

The girls sobbed.

"Sofia, honey, I need you to listen to me…"

As she spoke, she shifted her eyes to the metal bucket near the wall. Ramirez's people had delivered the bucket late last night and told her it was her toilet. They'd laughed. But Jackeline would have the last laugh.

———

A morning round of golf after a big breakfast always helped settle Jorge Ramirez's stomach.

He was expecting Fausto Sanchez to arrive, though, so he limited his play to the putting green. A golfer always needed putting practice.

Harry Donaldo stood off to the side acting as caddy. Ramirez tapped the ball and watched it roll across the green to the hole. It slowed, stopping short of the edge of the hole. Ramirez grunted. He reached out with the putter and pulled the ball back to him. A little more force. He addressed the ball once again, tapped, and the ball rolled straight into the hole with a satisfying plop.

"Good shot, jefe," Donaldo said.

Ramirez grunted. He bent to retrieve the ball. Donaldo's phone buzzed. He answered and directed the caller to the putting green. Ramirez set the ball further back and began the routine again, letting Donaldo deal with his incoming guest. Presently a golf cart rumbled across the grass with Fausto Sanchez in the passenger seat and one of his men driving. The golf cart stopped on the putting green. Sanchez stepped off. Ramirez watched as his man backed up, turned the cart the way they'd come, and rumbled off again.

"Having any luck?" Sanchez said. He jammed his hands into his pockets as he watched Ramirez tap the ball again.

"The routine is calming," Ramirez said. The ball stopped midway. "I'm having trouble controlling the force with which I hit the ball."

"I don't know anything about golf."

"You should try it." Ramirez lined up his next shot. *Tap. Plop.* He gestured for Donaldo to collect the ball while he sheathed the putter in the golf bag. He and Sanchez started walking back toward the main property.

"What is the latest?" Sanchez said.

"The women had a rough night," Ramirez said. "I kept them separated and let Jackeline wonder what we were doing with her kid."

"What did you do?"

"Nothing. Do I look like a monster?"

"We must make the tough decisions from time to time," Sanchez said.

"You'll learn as you get older," the old man said. "There are other ways. They've not had any food last night or today. I'm going to starve them for two days, and then Jackeline will do whatever we ask."

"Which is brutal in its own way."

"But smarter than torture, Fausto. Remember."

They crested a rise and approached the paved road stretching around the property. Loose gravel on the shoulder crunched as they stepped onto it. Ramirez said, "What about the Guardado place? Did the attack bring us a return on the investment?"

"We're still collecting items and data. There are rumors that leftover Guardado forces from processing plants and from the city may counter-attack, so I've dispatched teams to deal with them as well."

They crossed the road and stepped back onto grass. Ramirez kept the landscape conservative. Trimmed grass, bushes near building walls. The buildings themselves might have come from the same catalog; they looked identical, white stucco walls and brown tiled roofs. Only letters identified them, and each served its own purpose. Storage. Quarters for his men. Maintenance equipment for the grounds. The real toys were contained within the main house.

Sanchez continued, "There are many things of value at the mansion. We saved the family's horses as well. Carlos had a variety of cars. Do you want any of them?"

Ramirez shook his head. "You can have them all if you'd like."

"I would say," Sanchez said, "we've accomplished all of our stated goals and got rid of Manny Valdes at the same time. He was shot by Jackeline's bodyguard, we think."

"Doesn't matter. As long as he's dead. I've had Dante Costa disposed of, as well. It's all ours. We share with nobody."

Sanchez laughed. "Could we have planned it any better?"

"Fortune has favored us, yes," Ramirez said.

They continued toward the main house.

Stiletto wished he had some ear plugs.

The Huey helicopter was loud. They flew with the side doors open, the noise of the rotor blades numbing his ears. Temporary, sure, but it made for a long flight. He sat on the hard cabin floor with Victor Ramos, Amaya Olmos, Majors, Ellis, and McCoy. Two of Ramos's men filled the remaining space and they were crowded together. A second and third Huey flew alongside, their cabins containing more *El Tigre* shooters.

Ramos had given a good briefing, but the eyes of the *El Tigre* shooters across from Stiletto told another story. They looked wary, suspicious. Scott knew better than to focus on their questions; they had their orders whether they liked them or not. He wasn't the only one who didn't want to aid a known cartel leader while destroying another. He didn't blame them.

But the mission came before feelings. He'd finally cemented that fact in his own mind.

Victor Ramos wore a headset, and adjusted the connected microphone to respond to an incoming message. When he finished, he leaned toward Stiletto. He had to shout over the noise, but Scott understood him.

"Our forward scouts say it's all clear so far," the *El Tigre* leader said. "They report Fausto Sanchez arrived ten minutes ago."

"Two for one," Stiletto said. "I like it!"

Ramos smiled and sat back.

They'd land on the east side of the property near the

car park, and assault the property from there. The ground force would go in from the north side. The goal for Stiletto and his team was to get to Jackeline and Sofia and evacuate them from the scene. Ramos wanted to get into the main house and take out Ramirez, and now Sanchez, too, before they reached the alleged underground escape tunnel. Ramos had no problem with chasing them through the tunnel, but the unknowns of running underground prevented them from including a chase in the attack plan. Better to cut them off before they got there. A pursuit was an emergency option.

Stiletto looked out each of the open cabin doors. The other two Huey helicopters stayed on course with the main chopper.

Almost there.

Scott, as the chopper bumped with turbulence, decided something he hadn't considered since Jackeline and her daughter vanished. He had never wanted to accomplish a mission more than this one. Having overcome his prejudices, he truly wanted to see the Guardados find the peace they sought.

They'd earned it.

And he didn't want to fail them.

———

The door lock snapped back. A gunmen opened the door and stepped inside.

Jackeline stood behind the door, concealed behind it as the gunman pushed it open.

She held the metal bucket in both hands, ignoring the stench as it wafted under her nose.

Sofia stood in the center of the room, facing the door, her arms clasped behind her back and her chest puffed out. With the bottom of her shirt torn and her belly button and midriff exposed, the upward thrust of her T-shirt distracted the guard. He paused on the threshold and blinked.

"Where is your mother?" the gunman said. He pushed the door shut. As it swung back, Jackeline followed behind, and slammed the bucket over the gunman's head. The contents fell into his hair, rained down his neck and shoulders and the front and back of his shirt.

Jackline didn't stop moving. The gunner held his AK in his left hand, and she wrenched the rifle from the screaming gunner's grasp. She gripped it tightly and slammed the buttstock into the man's stomach. As he doubled over, she slammed the buttstock into his back. A sharp kick sent the bucket flying before he hit the floor, and Jackeline brought the stock down again, this time against the back of his skull. The gunner stopped screaming and didn't move.

Jackeline slung the rifle across her back and bent to unhook the gunner's chest rig of spare magazines. She donned it herself, tightening the straps over her frame. She unslung the Kalashnikov and checked the action. The gunner had the weapon on safe. She flipped the catch down to full auto and, lastly, removed the handgun from the man's holster. The pistol was a double-action Beretta 92FS, the bluing scuffed from hard use, but it appeared clean, oiled, and functional. She eased back the slide. A round sat in the chamber. She turned to her daughter.

Sofia stood with hands over her mouth, her eyes wide.

"We need to go, honey," she said. "Stay behind me. And take this."

She handed Sofia the handgun.

CHAPTER TWENTY-NINE

The Hueys dipped as they approached the Ramirez property. Ramos listened to messages on his headset; it wasn't hard to figure out what the ground force was telling him. They had begun the attack. Stiletto saw smoke and flames already happening on the property as the choppers neared. Ramos held up one finger. *One minute out.*

The Ramirez spread looked larger than Stiletto had figured. He spotted portions of the golf course, and several of the smaller buildings. Already troops were clashing, fighting, taking cover where available. Smoke was rising.

The Hueys swooped on over the parking lot on the east end. One opened fire with a heavy machine gun as two touched down. Stiletto and his crew raced out of the cabin, squinting against the dust kicked up by the whipping rotor blades. The choppers lifted off, the wind wake fading, and the third touched down. Sporadic shooting came their way as they ran across the pavement, a row of hedges coming up. Good

"But—"

"There's no time. Remember what I taught you. All you need to do is pull the trigger."

Sofia took the gun. Her hand was shaking.

"We're getting out of here, honey, come on."

concealment, lousy cover. But beyond the hedges lay the battle.

The choppers continued a sweep of the property, following a pattern as to not collide, and peppered the Ramirez troops with machine gun fire. The mounted US M60s hammered and spit lead as the door gunners fired controlled bursts, giving the *El Tigre* force an advantage over the Ramirez troops. The lead Huey also carried a pair of rocket pods, but Ramos had ordered the crew not to use the high explosive ordnance until he called for it.

An alarm began blaring throughout the estate, a high-pitched, piercing whine.

Stiletto took the lead, Amaya, Majors, and the other two Trust operatives behind him; the *El Tigre* element broke to the left, spreading out as they sought cover near buildings. They rounded the hedge, flanking several Ramirez gunners. Scott fired on the run, his M-4 popping, Majors joining in with his HK416. They skirted a fenced tennis court, beyond which lay a large swimming pool. The large building on the other side of the pool was the first structure they wanted to check for Jackeline and Sofia.

Bullets split the air, kicked up dirt around them. They spread out, taking up prone defensive positions, and returned fire. Stiletto called for Ellis and McCoy to continue their approach to the building. They acknowledged over wireless comm, and Stiletto fired single shots as they raced away. He hit one Ramirez gunner, who fell with a shoulder wound; he drove another gunner to cover. He was aware they had a portion of the Ramirez force squeezed between them and the *El Tigre* units, but the risk of friendly fire was now high. Stiletto radioed the chopper pilots to advise both parties of their proximity. Ellis and McCoy announced they'd gained the building. Stiletto told Amaya and Majors to break off next. He quickly changed magazines, and laid down more cover fire as they broke away.

Stiletto rolled left and crawled forward a few feet. As he sighted again, three Ramirez troops began a zigzag run to him. He shifted his aim and fired several shots, then blinked in surprise. A passing Huey left a long salvo of fire from the M60 door gun, and the trio twitched as the high-powered slugs ripped through their bodies. They collapsed in shredded heaps.

"We're ready for you, Scott," Amaya said over the comm.

Stiletto plucked a smoke grenade and rolled it ahead of him. As the smoke cloud bloomed, he took off at a sprint for the building he hoped Jackeline and Sofia were within.

———

Jackeline and Sofia ran hard. Jackeline kept looking back at her daughter, who kept up, but was already on the verge of panic. The intensity of the gunfire, the choppers, and rush of men, was more than Jackeline expected. She didn't know friend from foe. They ran for the main house and a cluster of sheds. Jackeline shot the lock off a narrow shed and rushed Sofia inside. She pulled the door shut and they both panted.

Jackeline looked around. Yard equipment hung on the walls. Sofia shrank back into a corner, gasping, sobbing; there was nothing Jackeline could do for her. She tried to catch her breath while gripping the AK in trembling hands; her legs felt like Jell-O but she forced herself to remain upright. Peering through cracks in the wall panels, she searched for a face she recognized. She moved about the shed, ignoring the alarm which grated on her senses, looking through cracks. Men raced by. The choppers roared overhead. They had a chance at rescue, but only a chance. They had a greater chance of being killed in the battle.

A bullet split the wood on one side; Sofia screamed. Jackeline told her to get flat on the ground. She spun, dropping to a knee; when a gunner jerked open the shed door, she didn't hesitate. The face was not familiar; he did not yell that he was with Ramos; he could only be one of Ramirez's men. She tightened her finger on the Kalashnikov's trigger and the rifle bucked in her hands. The blast blew the gunner back a step. He tumbled onto the ground. But more gunners saw her.

She crouched beside the door, flicked the selector to single shot, and began taking pot shots as the gunners dropped flat and rolled to avoid her shots. They didn't have much time to devote to her. *El Tigre* troops quickly moved in, and she held her fire. A swarm of slugs from *El Tigre* knocked down the Ramirez men as they tried to stand and run.

Jackeline sighted on the *El Tigre* men as they ran to her. One yelled that he was with Victor Ramos, and asked her name. Jackeline told him. She pointed to her daughter as well. The trooper keyed a radio and announced in rapid-fire Spanish he'd found the woman and child.

———

Stiletto and his crew were halfway through checking the building. It was a large gymnasium with basketball hoops, weight equipment, and showers. Stiletto knew they were in the wrong place, but kept up the search;

when the radio call announcing some of Ramos's men had found Jackeline, he called off the search. Amaya radioed back to keep Jackeline and Sofia covered while they went to join them. Stiletto led his people out of the building and back into the fight outside. Now they had to survive long enough to accomplish their mission.

CHAPTER THIRTY

The *El Tigre* soldier identified himself as Hermano; he told Jackeline they were going to take her to the road in front of the main house, where one of the choppers would pick them up.

Jackeline opened her mouth to respond, but then shrank back in horror as the front of Hermano's face split open. Blood splattered on her; she felt the bullet brush her cheek as it continued through. She stumbled, landed on her bottom with a painful cry, and crawled further back into the shed to shield Sofia. She leveled the AK at the open door.

Two other *El Tigre* troopers returned fire on unseen enemies, but it wasn't enough. One fell with a salvo of slugs tearing across his chest. The other pitched a grenade and dropped flat. As the blast detonated, the surviving *El Tigre* tried to fire again, but then the top of his head exploded and he fell flat.

Jackeline opened fire on targets she couldn't see. The AK clicked empty. She hurried to reload, dropping the fresh mag, scrambling to pick it up. The magazine slipped from her shaking hand again, and as she moved, she exposed Sofia.

The fifteen-year-old yelled, and Jackeline turned her head, holding a full mag in one hand and the empty Kalashnikov in the other.

"Shoot, Sofia!"

She dropped flat to avoid her daughter's fire.

"Shoot!"

Sofia thrust the gun out in front of her as Ramirez troopers approached the shed. The Beretta cracked repeatedly, the gun bouncing in the young girl's hand, none of the bullets firing true. She laid down enough lead to drive the gunners back, and Jackeline used the precious seconds to slap the full mag into the AK and yank back the charging handle. She stayed on the floor, rolling to aim the weapon out the door.

A crash of automatic weapons fire sounded from somewhere around the shed. The Ramirez gunners fell to the flesh-shredding slugs, and then Amaya ran into the shed and joined Jackeline and Sofia on the floor.

"We got you covered, Jackie, come on!"

Jackeline turned back to grab Sofia. The girl ran into her mother's arms. Amaya backed out of the shed and Jackeline and Sofia followed. She saw Stiletto and the rest of his team on the right side of the shed, covering them with their smoking weapons.

"Get her to the road!" Stiletto shouted.

Amaya led Jackeline and Sofia past the group, down the sloping grass to the frontage road passing the house. One of the Hueys flew overhead, machine guns blasting, and hovered over the pavement. The pilot set the chopper down, and Amaya ushered the pair aboard. She jumped in after them. The chopper lifted off again and flew away from the combat zone.

Stiletto looked back at the departing chopper. He felt relief despite the ongoing battle. Jackeline and her daughter were safe, out of danger, and now they had to finish the job.

"Let's find Ramos," he shouted. He ran for the main house with Majors, McCoy, and Ellis close behind.

———

Victor Ramos and a trio of his men stood guard as a fourth applied a charge to the front door of the main house. The battle raged. Two choppers remained in the fight, firing at the Ramirez men; his own forces continued sweeping the enemy fighters to the center of the property, picking them off as they gained ground. Smoke from fires drifted across the grounds, but the light wind kept it from concentrating in one area. Some of the smaller buildings burned steadily, adding to the smoke.

"Get clear!" the trooper shouted. He moved from the door and Ramos and the others followed. The blast broke the door from its hinges and it fell out of the doorway to land on the grass. Ramos ran through first; as his team followed, gunfire from inside rained down on them. Two fell. The last of the team fired back as they entered, and dodged left and right to avoid more fire.

They stepped into the arched-roof entryway. Lights above reflected off the marble tile, and curved staircases on either side led to a balcony overlooking the door. Ramos spotted the ambushing gunners on the balcony, and as his surviving fighters moved for cover, he ran under the overhang and plucked a grenade from his web vest. He stepped out far enough to pitch the grenade over the rail, and the blast shook the walls. He and his men ran up one side of the steps, firing on the staggering Ramirez troopers trying to retreat down a hallway. Two of the Ramirez gunners fell while another, as his rifle clicked empty, lunged at Ramos as he cleared the last step.

Ramos took the impact of the other man in the center of his torso. The momentum forced him back; he and the Ramirez trooper tumbled down the steps back to the entryway floor. Ramos landed beneath him, and the gunner punched him in the jaw. Ramos struggled to block follow-ups, but then the gunner snatched a knife from his belt and raised it overhead.

A gunshot cracked behind Ramos and the gunner's head snapped back. Ramos pushed the dead body off of him. As he rolled away and rose, he trained his weapon on the door, only to hold his fire as Stiletto, Ellis, and McCoy breezed inside. Majors, Ellis, and McCoy took a knee to cover Scott and Ramos as they hurried to the nearest wall.

"You hurt?" Stiletto said.

"I'm okay." Ramos radioed the men who'd gone upstairs to check for stragglers. He said to Scott, "We need to head for the tunnel. If we can beat Ramirez and Sanchez there—"

"Lead the way."

Ramos crossed the marble floor and paused beside a doorway. He checked around, announced it was clear, and Stiletto and his Trust associates hustled through.

———

Ramirez and Sanchez were already in the tunnel.

They'd evacuated to the escape route as soon as the shooting started. The tunnel led to a secondary garage on the west side of the property which was concealed from view, covered by treetops and vegetation around the building. Ramirez had a car ready there at all times.

They huffed and puffed as they half-ran the length of the tunnel, their shoes sluffing on the concrete floor. Lights on the walls lit the way, and anybody trying to follow into the tunnel after them would face a charge of C-4 sure to wipe them out.

"Almost there," Ramirez announced. Sanchez said nothing. A single gunman trailed behind them, looking back now and then, his AK at the ready.

The tunnel opened into the garage. Ramirez ignored the line of cars he'd amassed over the years and went straight to a black SUV. He and Sanchez and the gunner climbed in. The gunner took the wheel.

"Is it armored?" Sanchez asked.

"Are you kidding?"

The two men strapped on their seatbelts as the engine rumbled to life. The gunner put the car in gear and drove out of the garage into daylight.

CHAPTER THIRTY-ONE

Stiletto was the first to jump off the back of the deuce and a half as it rumbled into the *El Tigre* camp. His boots landed hard on the ground, and he pivoted to hurry past the vehicle to the main tent.

Amaya followed, and she ran past Scott to where Jackeline and Sofia waited within Ramos's tent. Stiletto didn't quicken his pace. He felt sweaty, dirty; *exhausted*. The last forty-eight hours had been intense, and the lack of proper sleep made his body ache more than it might otherwise have. His ears still rung from the gunfire and explosions, and he couldn't help feeling like a failure even though they'd rescued Jackeline and her daughter. Ramirez and Sanchez remained at large; their effort to chase them down had not been successful. A threat still hung over the Guardados and it weighed on his mind a great deal.

Jackeline and Amaya embraced; Amaya turned to Sofia, who refused to leave the corner chair she sat in with her arms folded and a faraway glaze across her face. Stiletto knew better than to bother her at this moment, and he put a hand on Amaya's arm to hold her back. She looked at him. He shook his head. She relaxed.

"What happened?" Jackeline said.

The rest of the Trust crew filtered into the tent, followed by Victor Ramos himself.

"We found the tablet in Ramirez's office," Stiletto said. "It's in one piece."

"Who has it?"

Ramos said, "I do," and produced the tablet from a pack. He handed it to Jackeline, who began examining the device. She made no comment on the state of the computer; it indeed appeared undamaged, albeit a little scuffed. She set it on one of the tables.

"I have men still mopping up," Ramos said, "but Ramirez and Sanchez escaped."

"They'd rigged the trap door for the tunnel with a bomb," Stiletto said. "We found it and tripped it, but the blast blew a bunch of concrete into the walkway. We couldn't get through."

Jackeline took a deep breath and folded her arms. "Now what?"

"We take you back to the States," Stiletto said.

"And Ramirez and Sanchez?"

Ramos said, "Leave them to me."

"They'll never stop trying to find us," Jackeline said.

"I know. They won't."

"Thank you for coming, Victor."

"How could I refuse?"

"Easily."

"I could never say no to you."

Stiletto turned to Majors. "Can you get the General on the phone and see about an extraction?"

Majors nodded and left the tent. Their Rover was nearby with the secure sat phone still inside.

Jackeline asked Ramos to join her on the other side of the tent, away from Stiletto and Amaya, Ellis and McCoy. They talked quietly. Stiletto looked at Sofia in the corner behind him. She was in shock, and deservedly so, and it wasn't his place to try and shake her out of it. Only her mother, and time, could heal whatever invisible scars she had after going through the battle. He wondered if there was something they could have done differently, such as leaving early, without dealing with Valdes, which was the only reason they'd waited. Leaving him for later might have been the better option, but it was too late now. They had to deal with the circumstances as they'd developed, and he hoped the girl didn't have nightmares the rest of her life.

If they didn't put a nail in the coffins of Jorge Ramirez and Fausto Sanchez, she might.

But they had to get them out of Colombia first. He'd be on the first plane back to link up with Ramos and *El Tigre* again to finish the job.

———

Jackeline said to Ramos, "I'm going to wire you money. It's the least I can do. Replenish your supplies."

"I won't argue," Ramos said. "I asked nothing of the Americans. I had no intention of asking anything of you. I don't know what you're doing, but it's not hard to figure out."

"I don't want my daughter living here. It's already too late to shield her from the worst but—"

"You did what you could. I wish you well. You'll always have a friend in Colombia. No matter what."

"I'm worried about Sofia."

"She is a brave young woman. She should be proud of herself."

"She hasn't said a word since we got on the helicopter."

"Give her time."

Jackeline shook her head. "I'll never forgive myself for this." She caught Amaya looking at her. She waved her over. Amaya walked around the tables to join them.

"What do you think?" Jackeline nodded at Sofia.

"Shock. It'll wear off."

"Speaking from experience?"

"Yes."

"Are you sure?"

"She'll be okay," Amaya said, "but it will take time. Being in a new place, where it's safe, will help."

Jackeline didn't reply. She watched her daughter with growing worry.

"Hey," Amaya said. Jackeline looked at her. "We're a family, remember? We'll help her adjust. And she'll never go through this again."

"I hope you're right," Jackeline said.

———

More of the *El Tigre* troops returned over the next few hours, most in trucks. Those who'd traveled in the choppers hitched a ride; the chopper pilots had returned the Hueys to a concealed airfield a few miles away. Stiletto wasn't sure where they were, but he was glad Ramos had the means to fly them.

He joined Majors at the Rover. The Trust operative was still on the sat phone, talking to General Ike. Scott waited for the conversation to conclude. When Majors hung up, he raised an eyebrow in question.

"We'll get a chopper pick up," Majors said. "I have to coordinate with Ramos. We'll need his landing spot, or find another. He may not want to share the exact location."

"We can only ask. If he refuses, we'll find another spot. Won't be hard."

"The boss said to tell you good job."

Stiletto scoffed. "We'll see about that. I just want to get out of here as fast as we can."

"You're not the only one."

CHAPTER THIRTY-TWO

A chopper flew them to Panama where they transferred to a private jet for the flight back to the United States. Stiletto, Amaya, and the rest of the Trust operatives had managed to change out of their combat gear, but everybody looked worn out. They made the transfer at a private airstrip far from any public eyes, and all Scott wanted was to sink into a padded leader chair, lift the footrest, and fall asleep for the rest of the flight home.

And he did.

When the jet touched down, the jolt of the landing shook Stiletto from his sleep. He looked around the cabin; he wasn't the only one stirring from a nap. He turned his chair to look out the side window. They had landed somewhere in the country. A green field, carefully cultivated, surrounded by thick trees. He frowned. The spot felt familiar. And then he saw a multi-story, white Victorian house in the center of the field. He smiled. He recognized the space because he'd been there before. The house had once been a headquarters for The Trust until cartel terrorists had struck; the place had been leveled in the ensuing battle. Scott remembered the General suggesting it would never be rebuilt, but apparently somebody decided otherwise.

Scott led the rest of the passengers off the plane. Meeting them on the tarmac was General Fleming himself, and a young blonde woman who grinned at Scott as he approached. She was Beth Carrington, and it felt good to see her back on her feet.

"Beth, how are you?"

"Much better."

Scott turned to Fleming. "Sir, let me introduce Jackeline and Sofia Guardado."

Fleming shook hands with Jackeline and greeted the still-sullen Sofia with a smile. The girl didn't respond, but instead cast her eyes around the vicinity. *Out of the frying pan, and into wonderland*, Stiletto thought.

"I didn't know the house had been rebuilt," Stiletto said.

"We'll use it for the debrief. It's private, quiet, and very comfortable. Who do we have here?"

Fleming shook hands with Amaya Olmos, whom Scott introduced, and Fleming ushered the trio into a golf cart which he drove back toward the house. Stiletto, Majors, Ellis, and McCoy looked at each other curiously; Stiletto said to Beth: "We have to walk?"

"We're short of golf carts," Beth said.

They started walking. Majors and Beth did most of the talking, with Stiletto listening, as she described what happened prior to her capture.

Stiletto half-listened. The remainder of his attention was focused on the quiet. Birds chirped; the fresh air felt good; knowing there was nobody in the tree line aiming a gun at him felt even better. His boots brushed the soft grass as they walked. He hoped the living quarters in the house, which he had briefly enjoyed when stationed here, retained their coziness, if by "cozy" one meant "cramped," but there had been a time when Stiletto thought the small room and bath was better than the most expensive hotel in New York City.

Beth nudged Scott with her elbow as they approached the house. "How did you get along with Jackeline?"

"Little rough at first," Scott told her without elaborating, "but we eventually connected. I'm concerned about her kid."

"That's up to Jackeline," Beth said. "We aren't shrinks, Scott."

Stiletto nodded and frowned at the same time. It was one thing to bring the Guardados over, but to abandon them after? Of course, it was typical of the spy business, but Stiletto hoped The Trust handled things better than their US government counterparts. He'd know soon enough.

"Is Carlos here too?" Stiletto asked.

"Yes," Beth said. "I'm sure they're going to be very happy within the next two minutes."

Stiletto hoped so. Jackeline and Sofia had been through too much to experience anything less.

———

Fleming let the two women enter the house ahead of him. They stopped in the entryway, looking to him for guidance, and he gestured to a sitting room off the entryway. He went ahead of them and entered first.

"Mr. Guardado," Fleming announced, "I have two people here who are very excited to see you."

Fleming stepped aside. Jackeline and Sofia rushed to

Carlos, who stood in the middle of the room. The three grasped each other tightly, Sofia crying, Carlos letting out his own joyous noises. Fleming watched with a satisfied smile. He didn't have to approve of their lifestyles—their former lifestyles—to know they shared the same concerns as any other family. As the group hug continued, he decided to step out and give them some privacy. They'd call for him when they were ready to talk about the next few days.

―――――

Fleming gave Stiletto and the team orders to get some rest and prepare for the next day, when the man known as Number One, commander in chief of The Trust, would join them at the house to discuss the operation.

Stiletto shut the door to his cramped room and stretched. Fleming told them everything they needed was in their assigned rooms. Scott checked the closet and found a change of clothes hanging there, along with the usual incidentals he required. They'd only be there overnight and part of the next day before heading back to Washington.

A shower was exactly what he needed. He climbed out of his clothes and stood under the hot spray in a daze for far longer than he intended; after soaping and rinsing rapidly, he pulled on a pair of boxers and stretched out on the bed. Within minutes he passed out.

―――――

General Ike Fleming returned to his own room after seeing Carlos and his wife and daughter have their first moments together since Carlos left Colombia. He did not want to intrude on the family, so he departed quietly. Carlos knew the sleeping arrangements and schedule for the next day. There was no reason for him to repeat any of the details, and if Carlos forgot, the General was willing to cut him plenty of slack and roust the family himself if needed.

He did ask Jackeline for her password to the tablet, and sat in his room going over her information with a growing sense of dread. He didn't recognize most of the names on the list of US officials receiving bribes from the Guardado Cartel, but he knew a few—and those names belonged to some of the top men in US law enforcement. When Number One arrived in the morning, they'd discuss the tablet over coffee. They had a lot of decisions to make.

————

Fleming and Number One held the morning meeting on the porch. Stiletto joined them, as did Beth and Mike Majors.

"Number One," the main man in The Trust, only called himself such as a cover. His real name was Edward Northwood. He was one of the three men who had formed the organization; someday Stiletto swore he'd meet the other two. Older than the rest, Number One addressed his people as they sat in a small circle on wooden chairs. Stiletto wished his chair had extra padding. He was already feeling uncomfortable.

"Has everybody had a chance to look at the tablet?" the old man said.

Fleming said no, explaining the security. Number One nodded, and began explaining to the agents what he and Fleming had found on the device.

"The individual drug agents and low-level officials won't mean anything to you," Number One said, "but there are some upper-level people on the list. And I'd like to ask Mrs. Guardado more about them."

"Tell us one," Stiletto said.

Fleming offered: "Tom Reynolds."

Stiletto raised an eyebrow. "The head of the DEA in Colombia? Stationed at the Embassy?"

"The same."

"It's a good thing he didn't know we were there," Stiletto said.

"Being outside the system has its merits, Scott," Number One said.

"You don't have to tell me, sir."

"We're dealing with a lot of people like Reynolds, those who took a bribe to look the other way instead of doing their jobs," Number One continued. "Our next question is, how do we best use this information to get what we want?"

"Which is what?" Stiletto said. He noticed Beth looking at him as he asked the question.

"We are in a tough spot, Scott. We have the Guardados. We can't do anything for them officially. Any form of witness protection isn't something we can set up. But if we tell certain people what information we're sitting on, we can use it to get them to help us."

Majors cleared his throat. Beth raised an eyebrow. Stiletto was the only one who had the guts to say: "Nuts."

Number One looked at him sharply. "What do you mean?"

"How do we know who we take into confidence won't run to his buddies who are on that tablet?"

Fleming jumped in. "There are some who are right-eous. We know who they are."

"Do we?"

"We have to have help, Scott. The only alternative—"

"Is to let the Guardados work out their future for themselves."

"Exactly."

"Which leaves them in danger. I know they have a backup plan, Jackeline told me, but I don't think it's any better than renting an apartment in downtown Los Angeles."

"We also have another chip to play," Number One said.

Stiletto and the others waited. A glance at Fleming told Stiletto the General already knew what the big boss was going to say.

"We still have Warren Hardison, the hacker," Number One said. "We've about obtained everything we need out of him, everything he has to tell us, and the CIA is still asking for their turn. I suggest we let them have him, and use the good will to further, shall we say, grease the skids in the Guardados' favor."

"I disagree, sir," Stiletto said.

Majors said, "Who is this guy?"

Stiletto gave Majors the rundown, including his role in capturing the hacker. "Surely Hardison is still of some use to us."

"We don't run a prison, Scott," Number One said. "What are we going to do with him indefinitely? I understand your hesitation, but it's what's best for Jackeline and her family. We need to try."

Stiletto took a breath to say something more, but held his words. He'd wanted to see The Trust do something different than leave the family out to dry; here he was throwing a wet blanket on the best ideas available to them.

"I'm sorry, sir, I withdraw my objections, you're right."

Number One nodded. "You are not wrong, but we simply can't carry on like our contemporaries."

"What do you need us to do to help?" Beth Carrington asked.

"For now, stand down here at the house, let's help the family adjust," Number One said. "We'll let you know when it's time."

And Stiletto knew the "time" for renewed action would arrive soon.

It was best to get some more rest in anticipation of the finale. There were a lot of names on the tablet, and every single one of them would want to protect themselves. And murder was but one of their options.

CHAPTER THIRTY-THREE

As soon as the Americans departed, Victor Ramos and his *El Tigre* force began packing to leave.

Ramos didn't think the Americans would betray him. Far from it, they'd keep his secrets forever. But he knew Ramirez and Sanchez wanted revenge. They'd turn up the heat and hunt for his crew sure as death and taxes, and they needed to be far away from their current base to prevent the cartel leaders from catching up. Ramos and his command team picked a new spot on the map fifty miles south, loaded up the trucks, and hit the road.

Ramos split the force into three convoys. The other two had gone via their own routes, and his followed another. Three big trucks, with him in the cabin of the lead vehicle, made their way through the jungle along a dirt road. The vegetation and tree cover were thick; only a hint of the blue sky above showed through the tree-tops. And all around them was enough cover to hide a superior force. Ramos checked his map and hoped they made the paved road five miles ahead soon. He felt like a sitting duck.

Sweat trickled down his neck and shoulder blades and had nothing to do with the thick humidity. There was a target on his back. But he had three trucks with a dozen men each; if the enemy wanted a fight, he had plenty of men to help give them one.

The convoy continued along the dirt road, the big, heavy tires carving deeper ruts into the earth than were there previously. The rumble of the engines made it hard to hear any incoming noises. Ramos feared helicopters more than foot soldiers. Choppers with machine guns and missiles, much like the ones he'd fielded, would make quick work of his convoy, and the others. They'd be reduced to piles of shredded metal and flesh within seconds.

Ramos glanced to his left. The young driver focused his attention on the road ahead, checking the mirrors, scanning for roadblocks. They also didn't need any fallen trees or boulders to delay their progress; so far, they'd been very fortunate not to encounter either. Ramos sighed. The young driver was young indeed, barely out of his twenties, and didn't belong with *El Tigre*. But he knew the young man's story as well as his own. He'd lost a sister and a fiancé to drug violence. He wanted payback like the rest. Ramos hoped, when the fight was out of him, when the bloodlust was satiated, if ever, he could return to a normal life. Ramos already knew it was too late for *him*; far too late to turn back now.

He knew better than to ask how much farther too. The distance was plainly obvious looking at the map. They had maybe another ten minutes before the tires would leave the dirt behind to finally touch pavement. There was nothing he could do to speed up the process.

He hoped the other two convoys reached the new camp safely. They had no radio contact for security reasons. Why let the enemy listen in? Like a worried father, Ramos wouldn't settle down until he saw his entire family together once again.

Presently he saw the break in the jungle. The road lay ahead. Sunlight streamed onto the pavement. His truck reached the road first, the young driver twisting the steering wheel to the left, the big truck following the turn. The driver pressed on the gas once all four wheels touched asphalt, and their speed increased. Jungle on one side and the other, no less danger than before, but Ramos was happy they were midway through their trip.

Now, instead of hiding within the foliage, an attack force might wait on either side of the road, hidden behind the heavy greenery, ready to light up the convoy with shoulder-fired missiles. Another trick Ramos had used before. There were far too many ways to accomplish their goal.

Ramos checked the mirror on his side. One, two. Both trucks accounted for. Now they had to stay together until they reached the new camp and reunited with their comrades in arms to continue the fight. Ramirez and Sanchez might have a target on *El Tigre*, but the reverse was true too. Ramos had no intention of walking away from the fight. He wanted to do his part to protect Jackeline and her family.

With a sigh Ramos folded his map and returned it to the front pocket of his uniform. His AK-47 lay with the buttstock on the floor and the business end resting against the seat. The barrel pointed at the roof. Not the safest way to leave a gun with a loaded mag and chamber, but it was there in case he needed it in a hurry.

The convoy rolled along at speed, maybe fifty-five or a little more, and Ramos began to think they were home free.

Mistake.

He didn't hear the chopper overhead, but the pilot messed up. He drifted to one side and the sun cast an obvious shadow of the chopper on the roadway.

Ramos yelled, "Chopper over us!"

Automatic weapons began popping behind him, his men firing out the back of the truck, those who were able anyway. They would be the ones closest to the opening at the rear. Ramos grabbed his AK as he looked left and right at each shoulder of the roadway, seeking some kind of cover for the trucks, but there were no openings the vehicles might pass through. And with the chopper overhead anyway, it was probably too late.

"Drive for your life!" he told the young man beside him.

The driver stepped harder on the gas and the truck surged forward.

But not as fast as Ramos would have liked.

The chopper flew over the convoy, ahead of Ramos's truck, and began to turn. Ramos leaned out his window with the AK-47 and opened fire, trying to hit the pilot, settling for any hit at all, but his rounds seemed to have no effect as the helicopter spun and headed back at them. The nose dipped low. Rockets flashed from pods under the short wings on either side, two contrails at the head of which were devastating warheads. Ramos pulled his upper body back into the cabin, for all the good it did, and uttered what he thought might be his final prayer.

The rockets struck the roadway short of the convoy.

As the twin blasts tore deep gouges in the asphalt and

sent chunks flying, the driver slammed the brakes. The truck's wheels locked and the rubber screeched until the big machine came to a stop at the edge of the damaged section of road. The windshield, peppered with debris, was a mass of spiderweb cracks. Ramos shouted for the driver and his men to get out and into the jungle. The only way to survive was to get out on foot. And even then, he wasn't sure they would all make it.

His feet hit the ground outside the cabin when another salvo of machine gun fire came from the chopper, the heavy slugs ripping into the trucks, shredding the canvas covering the rear bed, taking down some of his men as they tried to escape. Ramos heard their blood-curdling screams as he gained the jungle, diving into the foliage for cover.

He looked back. His men were following; some didn't make it. The next stream of machine gun fire from the chopper cut down more before they reached the tree line. Those who did survive dove for cover. Ramos's driver was close behind him, and Ramos shouted for the young man—*what was his name?*—to get his head down. He barely had the words out of his mouth when another machine gun blast smacked into the kid's back, opening him up like a jacket unzipped. He sprawled in a bloody mess on the jungle floor. *Poor kid never knew what hit him.* As Ramos shouted commands at his remaining troops, he tried to take solace in the fact the driver's death had been quick. Then he wondered if it even mattered.

Ramos ran deeper into the jungle, urging his men to follow. They did, catching up, spreading out in a loose formation of bodies to defend all sides. Ramos called a halt and he and his men flattened on the ground. The chopper hovered over the treetops, the whipping rotor blades almost drowning out Ramos's thoughts. The pilot and machine gunner might not be able to see them, but they knew they were somewhere below, and if ground troops came next, Ramos and his men would have their work cut out for them. The hard part was not knowing what to expect.

And then the first chopper pulled away, the rotor sounds fading as the helicopter left the area.

Ramos wondered what was happening. The faces of his men told him they had the same question. Ramos was afraid of the answer.

Then they heard the second and third choppers.

The noise of the twin engines increased intensity as the choppers landed on the road. Ramos saw the gleaming air machines touch down through gaps in the jungle. He didn't need to see more. He gestured for his men to spread out and get ready to engage. He didn't have to tell them twice. They swiftly blended into the green surrounding them, and Ramos didn't hold back a grin. His men were warriors. He'd trained them well.

They heard the approaching cartel troops before they saw them.

Ramos didn't need to tell his men what to do.

El Tigre opened fire, dozens of automatic weapons chattering at once, filling the jungle with a swarm of lead. The cartel troops not cut down by the intense fusillade dropped and rolled, but most of their comrades fell to the flesh-splitting slugs.

The survivors began throwing grenades.

As the explosive orbs completed their arc, Ramos rolled out of the way, yelling for anybody near him to get back and get down. He couldn't tell if anybody heeded his words. The blasts shook the ground. He felt the tug of shrapnel on his clothes but none of the deadly shards broke his skin. He rose a little, AK at his shoulder, and opened fire on targets of opportunity. It was tough to take aim with so much natural stuff in the way, but his rounds flew true, and he saw at least one cartel gunner fall to the 7.62x39mm rounds.

More shooting, fighting, and yelling filled the jungle. Some of Ramos's men and cartel troops engaged in hand-to-hand fighting, kicking, punching, stabbing, gouging; pistol shots settled a few of the fights, the screams of those run through with knives signaled the conclusion of others. Ramos changed magazines and kept moving, kept shooting, getting close to some targets while taking others from further away.

Ramos fought on autopilot, his vision clouded by the tunnel effect, his senses only taking in half of what was in front of him. He breathed hard and sweated harder, changing magazines as fast as he could when required, shooting, ducking, and blasting cartel troops about to shoot his men from cover positions.

As he slapped his final mag into the AK rifle, he stayed flat on the ground and took stock. He heard groans, cries; ground crunched as somebody moved; a pistol cracked. As his eyes darted left and right, Ramos felt a chill. There were less of his men and more of the cartel troops surrounding him now. He breathed slowly and dared not move a muscle. Men talking, talking about where he might be hiding, confirmed *El Tigre* had failed and the cartel had won this round.

What was left for him to do about the situation?

Die fighting.

He wasn't going to let the Ramirez and Sanchez forces take him alive. Capture meant humiliation. Better to go out with the last bullet than suffer the consequences of what the cartel leaders had in mind for him should they get hold of him.

He plucked a grenade from his web belt and set it on the soft ground before him. He removed another from his chest rig and pulled the pin. He waited.

Footsteps crunched to his left. He pitched the grenade he held that way, grabbed the second, pulled the pin. When the blast came, men screamed, and he tossed the second grenade to his left to catch any stragglers. He was on his feet and running when the second blast split the afternoon. He fired to his left, then right, using only a couple of rounds to conserve his ammo. Then he spotted a dip in the ground with enough of a rise to provide a place for a last stand. He ducked and rolled down the rise, bottoming out, then propped himself up to fire over the rise as the cartel forces closed in.

They approached in a wide line, closing like hungry sharks, each one determined to get the kill. Ramos opened fire. The brass ejecting from his AK landed in the dirt to his right, the cases clinking as they collided, sweat dripping into his eyes as he sought targets from the smoking muzzle of his rifle.

Bodies dropped; men cried out; others rushed forward to finish the job.

The AK clicked empty. Ramos grabbed for his pistol. Then they were on him. He shot one in the face, missed another, and was swinging the barrel wildly to bash some heads when they were on him en masse, slamming buttstocks into his body, pummeling him into a bloody, unmoving pulp. When one called for an end to the beating, the speaker shot Ramos in the head. Ramos was already gone. They couldn't kill him more than once.

Two of the cartel troopers knelt beside Ramos to search his body for anything of interest. They found a pocket-sized leather-bound journal.

The cartel killers frowned as the gunner who had given the order to stop the beating stepped back. Blood spotted the front and back covers of the journal. The gunner began to read. Others read over his shoulder. As the words on the pages sank in, they all knew the journal was something Ramirez and Sanchez would very badly want to see.

———

"The men did well," Ramirez said into the phone.

"Was there any doubt?" Fausto Sanchez asked.

Both cartel leaders had retreated to their individual hideouts, Sanchez back to his own palatial estate, while Ramirez took refuge at a backup location. It wasn't as nice as his other estate. No personal golf course this time. But it was a place to hide while his other home was cleaned and rebuilt. He didn't want to go back until all the necessary repairs had been completed. He wanted to see no sign of a war when he returned.

Ramirez held the still-a-little-bloody leather-bound notebook in his hand. He'd read enough to know it was Ramos's personal diary, or at least part of a regular set of journals he kept, but the most recent entry held the most important information. Especially the last pages.

"They brought back something we need very much," Ramirez said. "This is better than taking Ramos alive. It answers our questions."

"In how much detail?"

"Enough to fill the gaps on what we've already decided was the truth," Ramirez said. "Ramos has his own speculation, saying Jackeline Guardado didn't give him any specifics, and neither did the American, but to his thinking she and her husband have defected to the

United States like a KGB agent might have done back in the old days of the Cold War."

"I wasn't even born then, Jorge."

Ramirez almost laughed, but didn't. His partner in crime suddenly made him feel old.

"What it means is they are now on US soil, and we need to do something about this."

"What do you suggest?"

"Send the word out. Let our people in the US know what's going on, and tell them to be on the lookout. When they find Carlos and Jackeline, we need to know. And we need to make sure we have people ready to do what is required. Surely, we have some capable killers in the US already, do we not?"

"I have a few," Sanchez said. "Only you can answer your side of the question."

"When they find them, we can be finished with this chapter once and for all. Then there will be nothing left to stop us."

"Is the tablet still a priority?"

"If they can find it, yes. If not, we will have to find a way to live without it."

CHAPTER THIRTY-FOUR

Stiletto felt funny wearing a suit and tie, but the restaurant had a strictly-enforced dress code. He didn't want to get into a boxing match with an overeager maître d'.

He also didn't want to attend the meeting, but, as had been a common theme of late, orders were orders. He was the man most familiar with the material. It might have been nice to have General Ike or Number One along with him, but they had to tend to the Guardados at the Blue Ridge facility and continue the debriefing. Scott was on his own, but he didn't think he'd have any problems.

He drove into downtown DC and entered Mastro's Steakhouse, whistling as he took in the fancy décor. The dining area featured crystal chandeliers, high quality checkered carpet, and a quiet clientele. This wasn't the kind of restaurant for loud parties.

He said he was there to meet Mr. Robert Mason, and the young hostess, who checked out his suit with a raised eyebrow, escorted him through the busy restaurant. She didn't bar his entry so apparently the suit passed muster, despite its off-the-rack heritage. He quickly realized no other men in the place wore anything less than a fully tailored, bespoke suit, and he recognized a few faces as well. Nobody who would know him in return, but the faces he noticed belonged to the DC elite, some of whom mixed cordially with bitter rivals if the news programs were to be believed. Stiletto wasn't surprised. He never put much stock in anything the media said or advocated. He knew too well how most of it was "spun" for the benefit of somebody else. And political arguments between career politicians were often nothing more than Kabuki theater.

He even noticed one or two big shots with their actual wives. Wonders never ceased!

The hostess brought Scott to a table near the back, around the corner from the bar. Sitting with his back to the wall was FBI Director Robert Mason. The chief G-man stood as Stiletto approached. Scott thanked the hostess, shook hands with Mason, and both men took a seat. Stiletto felt odd with his back exposed, but a quiet dinner usually wasn't a prelude to combat. *Usually*.

"Just so you're aware," the FBI man said, "I have my bodyguards over there and over there." He gestured with his eyes. "Don't want you to be surprised by anything."

"No problem." Stiletto didn't look for the muscle. There were enough other tables nearby, and space at a minimum, to make a fight difficult to manage. Besides, who'd want to wreck such a nice restaurant?

"I've heard a lot about you, Mr. Stiletto."

"Some of it is probably true."

Mason laughed. He said, "I've also heard a little about what you're here to talk to me about. It sounds disturbing."

"It is."

Scott didn't have Jackeline's tablet on him, but he did have printouts to show the FBI director what was on the device.

Their waiter arrived and both ordered drinks, Mason choosing a double scotch since he wasn't paying. Stiletto ordered a gin and tonic with a slice of lime. They made small talk, Mason asking about Stiletto's time at the CIA and did he know so-and-so. Scott answered what wasn't sensitive or classified. Mason didn't probe too deeply, and seemed genuinely interested.

Finally, halfway through his Johnny Walker, Mason came to the point of the visit.

"Do I want to see this information now, or wait?"

"Might ruin your appetite if you see them now."

"I've been in charge of the FBI for fourteen years. If I let every piece of bad news keep me from eating, I'd starve to death. What do you got?"

Stiletto set his glass down and reached into his jacket. He pulled out several folded sheets of paper. Each contained a screen shot of what Jackeline had on her tablet. Scott and General Ike had made sure the names of US officials were on the pages, but he had a few showing Colombian officials, too, to balance out the story.

Mason took his time reading, examining each name, amounts paid, how often they were paid, and by whom. He knew the Guardados were in the US and how The Trust had brought them there. Number One had known Mason when they were both younger, so the meeting hadn't been difficult to set up. Scott was there to provide full context, answer questions, and let Mason know what The Trust needed next. The goal was to trade the information on the tablet for a witness protection deal. It was the only way Number One and

General Ike felt they could keep their promises to the family.

"Wow," Mason said as he read. "We knew none of this. Then again, we also weren't looking. Or paying attention."

"You can't police everybody. Not with your workload."

"I appreciate the benefit of the doubt."

"I'm not blowing smoke up your ass. We know how it is. Nobody's blaming anybody."

"But I hate to learn this after they've done so much damage." Mason read a second sheet, then a third. He looked at the list of Colombian names but admitted he only recognized one name from a visit to the country several years earlier.

He set down the pages and swallowed more scotch. Stiletto figured he probably had wished for a triple. He flagged down their waiter for refills.

Mason handed back the papers and said he needed time to think. Stiletto sat without talking and gave him the time, which was interrupted by a passing man, wearing a similar suit to Mason's, who stopped by to say hello. Mason did not introduce the man to Scott, who also didn't ask.

"How much do you have?" Mason said.

"Quite a bit more."

The waiter returned for their dinner orders; Mason recommended the 8 oz. filet mignon if Scott wanted a lean cut. Scott examined the menu again. The 8-ouncer was actually one of the less expensive items on the menu at a flat sixty dollars. The eighty-seven dollar "Chef's Cut" rib eye chop sounded tempting, but he didn't want to bankrupt Number One, after all. They both ordered the filet and a couple of large side dishes to split.

"What do you want?" the FBI man said. "In return, I mean."

"The Guardados need a spot in WITSEC."

"You think I can arrange that with some of the names on this list? They'll be blown before we ever put them in the system."

"Keep those people out of it then."

Mason nodded. "Be a bit tougher, but not impossible. I'd still be afraid of somebody finding out after the fact."

"Surely—"

Mason interrupted. "I can only use the evidence you're bringing as support," he said. "I'd need to build this case, or rebuild it, from the ground up. Start fresh on our own. It won't happen overnight."

"Apply pressure to those names," Scott said, "and they'll make the case for you."

"I'll need to show where the tip came from. Let me ask you this. Will the family be willing to testify? If I can put the Guardados on the stand—"

"You were saying about the risk?"

Mason sighed. "Our mutual friend," he said, "told me what they've done. I checked out his claims too. They've done some good work. We knew you people were making strong headway; now we know how."

"And they deserve our help in getting a new start," Scott said.

"I'm not arguing. What I'm not sure about is how to make this happen."

"You get the tablet, they get WITSEC." *How hard does he have to make this?*

"Can you ask about testimony? We can keep them anonymous, shielded, stuff like that."

"I can ask whatever you want. I wasn't told to say no to anything. But that family needs to disappear. Either we help them and benefit, or they take off on their own and we get nothing but the tablet."

"How do they intend to vanish without a trace?" Mason said.

Stiletto shrugged. "All I know is they have a backup plan in case we fail them."

"I can keep the circle tight, use people I trust who aren't on this list."

Now we're getting somewhere. "You should see the whole thing before forming your circle, Mr. Mason."

"No doubt. Boy, I need another drink."

Their food arrived and they took a few minutes to eat and compliment how well the chef cooked the filet. Mason assured Scott the chefs were very consistent and he never had a bad meal. Scott took his time with each bite.

"Can I talk to them myself?" Mason said. "You know, arrange a secret meeting? Just me, nobody else."

"I'll find out."

"We can make this work. We *must* make this work. This level of corruption—my goodness, if this leaks to the press, confidence in US law enforcement will take another hit. We don't need any more bad press than we already get."

"And most of it undeserved."

"Tell me about it."

Stiletto liked Mason, and hadn't expected to. He figured anybody friendly with Number One was probably okay, but Number One had associations with many people, and not all of them were friendly toward what The Trust represented or carried out. Mason knew a good thing when he saw it; or, in this case, a bad thing; he also knew not to shut them down or let them go. He saw the value in what Carlos and Jackeline Guardado had brought from Colombia.

They finished eating but passed on dessert. Mason said he wanted to get home and do more thinking. He asked Scott to make sure and ask the questions he wanted answered, and Stiletto made a note on his phone. He didn't want to let the FBI man down by forgetting.

Stiletto used the credit card given to him by the General to pay, and walked Mason to his car. They shook hands and said good night. Stiletto went to his own car feeling a genuine sense of accomplishment. They'd keep the promise. It was the least they could do for a family who had sacrificed everything after five years of service.

———

Stiletto returned to his apartment and climbed out of the suit and tie first thing. Then he grabbed a beer from the refrigerator and stood in the kitchen to call the General.

"Success?" General Ike asked.

Stiletto gave him the details of the meeting and Fleming agreed they should talk to the Guardados about the FBI's needs first thing in the morning.

"Fine with me, sir," Scott said.

"Get some rest. We have other matters to address tomorrow too."

"You mean Hardison."

"We're giving him to the CIA as an act of good faith. We'll also need their help with the Carlos and Jackeline situation. I'd like you there when we do the handoff."

Stiletto sighed.

"I know you don't like it—"

"I haven't liked *any* aspect of this mission, sir. But you can count on me. I will see you in the morning."

They ended the call and Stiletto stood in the kitchen a long time to not only finish his beer, but reflect. He decided he'd have a lot to tell Doctor Gargarin when they next saw each other.

———

"We meet again."

Stiletto raised an eyebrow at Warren Hardison as he climbed into the back of the Town Car. The hacker sat between him and General Ike, wrists held together with a zip tie, dressed in the same suit he'd been captured in. Scott noted somebody had cleaned and pressed the suit, at least. Hardison's formerly perfect hair, however, had grown wild since their last meeting. Nobody had bothered to give him a comb. Scott buckled his seat belt.

"Good morning, Mr. Hardison," Stiletto said. He pulled the back door shut.

"You guys aren't FBI," the hacker said.

"What gave it away?" General Ike chimed in. Stiletto grinned at the boss's snark.

Hardison only scoffed in reply. The driver asked if they were ready, the General said yes, and the driver put the car in gear and drove. They were on their way to the meeting point where representatives of the CIA waited.

They drove through DC and onto the Beltway, heading south for Maryland. Scott wasn't aware of the final destination. He also wasn't sure why the General insisted of him being there, but figured the boss wanted some security. He was armed in case of trouble. He toted not only his Colt pistol, but a compact HK SMG under his coat. The HK MP5K, with its folding stock reducing the overall size, wasn't much bigger than a large hand-gun. It wasn't a comfortable fit while seated in the back seat of a Town Car wedged against a prisoner, but Scott adjusted. He questioned the need for heavy artillery for what was a meeting between two teams on the same side, but, hell, they were dealing with the CIA. One could never be too careful. He'd been one of them once. He knew how they thought. Sometimes, in such meetings, it was tempting to make the other side vanish so nobody knew what had happened. Then again, his meetings had always involved potential enemies, never fellow citizens or "agents" of an unofficial organization.

He supposed it all depended on whether they were upset about being outbid for Hardison's device.

"Why can't you people," Hardison said, "hand over transcripts or something? Why do I need to be grilled all over again?"

"They have their own questions for you," General Ike said. "Besides, what's the alternative? We aren't going to let you go, you know."

"A concrete overcoat is preferable to being shuffled between agencies and asked the same things over and over again," the hacker said.

"We thought of that," the General replied, "but we didn't have your size."

"Budget problems?"

"Or something," Fleming managed to reply.

Stiletto remained quiet. If he was there for security, he might as well act like security. He watched the road, the traffic, the environment around them, looking for anything out of the ordinary. Threats, potential traps, anything the CIA might have engineered to make sure their drive wasn't peaceful.

Good grief, somebody's paranoid, he thought.

After an hour the driver pulled off the freeway and spent another few minutes navigating city streets, until he pulled into a parking area with a cluster of warehouses, most of which looked empty. Were they trying for the "For Lease" trick same as The Trust? Scott had no idea, and didn't ask the General, who might have known the answer. He saw two cars and four men not far away, and relished the idea of being done with the Hardison case once and for all. Let the CIA have their way with him, and give him the exit he wanted, if he wanted it badly enough. Stiletto didn't think he'd have much of a future no matter what happened. But it wasn't his concern any longer.

The Town Car stopped. General Ike and Stiletto exited as one of the CIA representatives approached. Stiletto smiled. At least they'd sent somebody he knew. David McNeil had once been General Ike's number two at Special Activities, and he shook hands warmly with the General before doing the same with Scott.

"Good to see you both," McNeil said. "I'm glad the two of you are still causing trouble."

"You should join us," Stiletto said. Fleming gave him a look.

"You can't afford me," McNeil said. They laughed. "So where's the—"

"In the car, David," Fleming said. He leaned into the Town Car and told Hardison it was time to get out. When the hacker hesitated, Stiletto took the General's place and grabbed Hardison's arm. The hacker scooted across the back seat and stepped out. McNeil gestured for two of his men to come over. The new arrivals may have worn suits, but Stiletto knew hardened killers when he saw them, and the two CIA men grabbed Hardison roughly and dragged him to their car, where they stuffed him inside.

"Thank you, General," McNeil said.

"Thank *you*, David."

McNeil shook Stiletto's hand again. "We need to catch up sometime."

"I hope so."

Fleming and Stiletto climbed back into the Town Car. The driver made a U-turn and drove away. Scott looked back to see McNeil watching them leave.

"Sir," Stiletto said, turning forward, "why don't we have David on our side?"

"He's more valuable to me at CIA."

"To *you*?"

"He managed to avoid the firestorm which resulted in my dismissal," the General explained. "And he passes along bits of information he thinks I might find interesting. You know, now and then."

"Can you anticipate my next question?"

Fleming cracked a grin. "Go ahead."

"When we were bidding for the Hardison device, did we know we were offering more than CIA?"

Fleming's grin broke into a smile.

"David told you their bid, didn't he?"

"He did."

"Yet now they're getting Hardison for free."

"It's a goodwill gesture. They get Hardison; we got the device, which we destroyed, by the way."

"Because?"

"Don't want it falling into the wrong hands. But back to Hardison himself. We can't keep him detained indefinitely, and we got to him first, so we get the satisfaction of beating the CIA, but now they owe us a favor."

"I'm sure you'll call for it soon."

"Depends. Knowing they know they owe us is satisfaction enough."

Stiletto laughed. The spy business. It never failed to amaze him the strange bedfellows the business produced.

"Well, good. I like having a rooster in the henhouse."

Fleming changed the subject. "Are you ready for this afternoon?"

It had been a busy morning. Stiletto not only had to get ready for the Hardison exchange, but FBI Director Mason reached out to him as well. He knew how to get the Guardados into protective custody, and wanted them under the WITSEC umbrella right away. After lunch, Stiletto and Fleming and Mike Majors would be on their way back to the safe house in the Blue Ridge Mountains to collect the family and bring them to a federal safe house where the entry process would begin, and their new lives. Stiletto, after so much agony over the mission, was glad they'd finally receive what had been promised to them so long ago.

"It will feel good to be done with this project, General."

"Indeed, it will. I know how tough it's been for you. You have my gratitude for seeing it through."

Stiletto wasn't sure what to say.

The driver merged onto the freeway and began the drive back to Washington, DC.

CHAPTER THIRTY-FIVE

Taking a helicopter to the Blue Ridge site beat the heck out of driving.

Too bad they'd have to drive off the property to their next destination. The chopper didn't have room for everybody.

Stiletto and Mike Majors hopped out of the chopper. Beth Carrington waited for them in a golf cart. They climbed aboard. As she turned the cart around for the short ride to the Victorian, the chopper lifted off the landing pad and departed over the trees.

"Are they ready?" Stiletto asked.

"Cautiously optimistic is how I'd describe them," Beth said. She looked well after her ordeal in Colombia; rest and light duty agreed with her. But Scott knew Beth too well. She'd be chomping at the bit to get back into action. She'd wait until the time was right, however. She wasn't like him, who'd dive back into the fire while still wearing bandages.

The cart rolled over the bumpy ground. Stiletto and Majors held on while Beth gripped the wheel. Armed sentries covered various points around the Victorian. Scott knew there were others, unseen, also keeping watch. The surrounding trees might suggest tranquility, but men with guns ready to defend the property with violence lurked within.

"How's Sofia holding up?" Stiletto asked as they neared the house.

"Very well. Being back with her father has helped."

She stopped the golf cart at the steps of the porch and shut off the power. The trio left the cart and climbed the steps into the house. Stiletto looked forward to seeing Carlos Guardado again. He'd only managed a quick hello when the family was reunited. He deserved to know how well his wife and daughter handled the pressure in his absence.

Beth led him and Majors into a sitting room where the Guardados and Amaya Olmos waited. Carlos jumped from a seat to shake Stiletto's hand.

"I didn't get a chance to properly thank you," the former drug baron said.

Stiletto said, "You're welcome. Your wife and daughter are real fighters."

Jackeline, standing nearby, didn't blush, but looked away a moment before giving Stiletto a casual embrace. Carlos turned his attention to Mike Majors.

Amaya sat with Sofia on a couch. Stiletto went over to them.

"You doing okay, Sofia?"

She only nodded.

Amaya put an arm around the girl and squeezed. "She's going to be fine. She has her father back."

Sofia smiled.

"I hope you understand why your mother had to keep this a secret," Stiletto said.

"I'm still processing," Sofia said. "But I think I get it."

With the greetings finished, Stiletto asked for their attention.

"Here's the situation," he said. "The FBI has agreed to give you witness protection in exchange for the information on Jackeline's tablet. They may need your personal testimonies in any trials resulting from their investigation, but they can keep you hidden from view and scramble your voices to keep your identities secured.

"Agents are waiting at a safe house in DC," he continued, "so we have a bit of a drive ahead. But they have new identities and details about your new lives waiting for you."

Carlos said, "We have hidden assets in the United States."

"You will not be stopped from accessing those assets, Carlos."

"This is in writing?"

"I don't have any documents, but the FBI does. My team and I won't depart until you're satisfied. Failing that, you come back here until we get it worked out. But I have the FBI director's word what you want is in order and ready for you to sign."

Jackeline said, "So we sign those papers—"

"And you'll be relocated. They'll give you a few options on where you want to go."

"Amaya is included?" Jackeline said.

"Amaya is included," Stiletto promised. He looked at Jackeline's bodyguard for a reaction, but Amaya remained stoic. She wouldn't believe Scott until she saw the documents for herself. Or maybe she'd learned the hard way to keep her emotions subdued. Either way Stiletto had hope she'd learn to relax and enjoy peace for a change, in whichever part of the country the family decided to settle.

"There's one other thing," Stiletto said. He pulled from his back pocket a cell phone. Jackeline being closest to him, he handed the phone to her. "Pre-paid phone. My number is stored. If you ever need anything, you call me. Got it?"

She nodded and put the phone in a pocket of her jeans.

Carlos said, "We appreciate everything."

"And we appreciate what you've done for us and the drug war, such as it is. Maybe the information on your tablet will help us close down a few more pipelines into the US and Europe."

"And we will be available to testify," Carlos added.

"You don't need to convince me," Stiletto said. "It's up to you. With the information available, the FBI can prove their cases with or without you, but being willing to provide your own statements might help them move things along. Shall we get going?"

Two black armored Suburbans with tinted windows pulled around to the front of the house. The family went into one, Stiletto and Majors and Amaya into the other. Stiletto showed Amaya how to free the Heckler & Koch MP7 submachine guns secured in the doors. Before she climbed into the back, she kissed him on the cheek. He cracked a small smile, but she added nothing as she entered the vehicle. He followed behind her.

The two Suburbans left The Trust installation and headed for a dirt road in the forest. It was a slow drive to the highway, but then the drivers picked up speed and headed for DC.

———

They drove to Georgetown, Stiletto wishing the community with its cozy neighborhoods and cobble-stoned streets was merely a tourist stop for the Guarda-dos. They drove past the main streets and drove deeper into a neighborhood of close-packed homes. Nobody paid attention to the blacked-out Suburbans. They were government cars in a government town and a familiar sight, but Scott still felt nervous when they reached their final destination. Anybody watching for said vehicles, and their VIP cargo, might be calling for a hit team to move in at any moment.

The safe house at least looked nice on the outside. Made primarily of red brick, it occupied a small space on its lot, surrounded by trees which blocked the windows, and a brick wall dividing it from neighbors. Stiletto and Majors exited first, checked to make sure the street was clear, and gestured for Amaya and the Guardados to step out. There were plenty of other cars lining the street, but they all appeared unoccupied, not threatening. It was the rooftops of the other homes Stiletto had his eye on. A sniper might find said rooftops a convenient place to hide. He knew enough about the subject to feel certain.

Majors had the front door of the home open before the family exited, and Stiletto ushered them up the steps and into the house. He was the last one to step through the doorway. He closed the door behind him. The drivers of the SUVs remained out front with the engines running. Stiletto and Majors weren't intending to stay long.

Stiletto handled the introductions with the FBI people, and remained long enough to review the WITSEC documents with the Guardados to ensure the FBI was keeping its word, and all of their requests were covered. When it was finally time to leave, Stiletto said good bye with genuine regret. Despite himself, he had grown fond of the Guardados, and Amaya Olmos too. They said their good byes with handshakes and hugs and Scott and Majors departed. Climbing back into the Suburban they'd arrived in; they told the driver to get going. The other SUV followed.

And that was it. Mission accomplished. Stiletto let out a heavy sigh and Majors agreed.

"Tough nut," Majors said.

"But it's over now. They're on their own now whatever happens next."

"They'll be fine."

"I'm going to ask the driver to let me off at my apartment. Care to join me for a beer to celebrate?"

"I couldn't think of a better idea," Majors said.

———

Jackeline Guardado didn't feel comfortable at all.

You're only nervous, she told herself. She stayed close to Sofia at the big kitchen table while she and Carlos reviewed the documents they'd signed, as if looking for a trap once the danger had ceased. Stiletto had said all was well; she believed him, but couldn't fight lingering doubts. The men around her regarded them neutrally, but she wondered what they were thinking.

There were two FBI agents in suits who did all the talking, and three FBI agents in combat gear carrying submachines guns stationed around the living room. The "safe house" might easily be a coffin if they decided to kill them.

Stop it!

Carlos must have sensed the tension inside her, because he grabbed one of her hands and squeezed. She squeezed back. Some of the pressure left her mind; some remained. She glanced at Amaya, who remained standing in a corner, but read nothing in her bodyguard's weary face. Seeing Amaya without a weapon, not even a handgun on her belt, actually troubled her for a moment. She'd have to get used to the idea of not seeing weapons on a regular basis. She decided it would be nice once she adjusted.

One of the FBI men at the table said, "I hate to keep shuffling the four of you in and out of cars, but we don't want to keep you here very long. We have a secure site at Quantico waiting for you. That's our training facility. You'll have more armed guards than you've probably ever seen."

"Why didn't we go there to start?" Carlos said.

"It was my boss's decision. This is a halfway point between wherever The Trust had you and us."

Carlos frowned. Jackeline didn't like the frown.

The agent checked his watch. One of the sentries peeked out a window.

"Cars are here," the sentry announced.

"That's our ride," the agent said, rising. "I'll go out first and then my team—"

A bomb went off.

The blast occurred in another room in the house, but it was enough to shake the walls, cracks appearing in the sheetrock. Windows shattered, and Carlos Guardado dove for his wife and Amaya Olmos pushed Sofia under the dining table.

The FBI men began shouting as the front door crashed open and black-clad gunmen filed inside, submachine guns chattering without the benefit of sound suppressors. Agents dropped with lines of bullet holes across their chests or returned fire from cover. The house filled with the ear-splitting cracks of gunfire. Jackeline, under the table, huddled close to her daughter and husband.

She didn't panic. She was surprised at how calm she felt, as if her worst fears had been realized, and she was back on familiar turf, defending her life and the lives of her loved ones from those who wanted to take them. She grabbed for the cell phone Stiletto had given her. His number was the only one stored. She pressed CALL.

He answered.

She shouted, "It's a set up! Get back here!"

CHAPTER THIRTY-SIX

The Suburbans screeched to a halt outside the red brick safe house.

"Don't shoot any FBI guys!" Stiletto shouted as he and Majors exited, taking with them the HK MP7s from the interior door mounts.

They rushed up the steps to the open door. Smoke billowed outside. Sirens in the distance signaled approaching police and emergency crews; they had to act fast. Stiletto didn't want to leave the Guardados at a compromised location. If they were still alive. He hoped they weren't too late.

Gunfire crackled from inside as they cleared the doorway with the MP7s at the ready. Targets offered themselves immediately, black-clad gunmen who in no way looked like the FBI people either on the floor bleeding or firing from cover. Their faces were covered; their tactical gear had no government identification markings. *Open season*, Stiletto thought, as his finger stroked the MP7s trigger.

The submachine gun bucked against his shoulder as

the salvo left the muzzle, the tri-burst of high-powered slugs tearing through the gunman's gear and plowing through soft flesh. The gunman let out a scream as he tried to turn to face the new threat. Stiletto's follow-up burst ripped a chunk out of his throat and he collapsed to the floor.

Mike Majors sighted on the second gunman; he fired a single shot into the man's head, decorating the wall behind him with a splash of red and bits of bone. Second gunman down.

"How many more!" Stiletto shouted as he advanced into the house.

"Only the two!" somebody shouted back. Stiletto recognized the voice of the FBI agent in charge. He'd forgotten the man's name.

"Amaya!" Stiletto shouted. "Amaya!"

"Here!" The Guardados' bodyguard rose from under the dining table.

"Get everybody out to the SUVs! Now!"

Amaya hustled Carlos, Jackeline, and Sofia from under the table. She hustled them past Scott and Majors and outside.

"Mike!"

"With them!"

Stiletto kept up a danger scan as Majors exited. He started backing up to the door.

"You can't take them!" the FBI man shouted. He approached Stiletto with his hands open and empty. "They're our responsibility now!"

"You're compromised!" Stiletto yelled back. He turned through the doorway and jumped into one of the SUVs. The drivers didn't waste a second. Before Stiletto had his door shut, the vehicles were on their way, tires screeching, leaving behind a patch of rubber in the asphalt.

Stiletto, breathing heavily, looked around. He was in the second Suburban with Carlos and Jackeline. Sofia and Amaya and Majors were in the first vehicle.

"So much for your FBI!" Carlos shouted.

"No shit," Stiletto told him. "The leaks are worse than any of us thought."

"Now what?" Jackeline said. Stiletto saw the strain in her eyes.

"I think now," he said, "it's up to you. Can you disappear like you said?"

Jackeline looked at her husband. Carlos nodded at her. To Scott, he said, "We can do it."

"But we'll need your help," Jackeline added.

"Why?"

"The cash we have," she said, "is probably too risky to go for right now. But we have gold."

"Gold?"

"Bars of gold hidden in Nevada," she said. "If we can get to it, we can pull our Houdini act. Will you go with us?"

"You don't have to ask," Stiletto said. "I can't speak for Mike but I'm sure he'll agree. Between him and me and Amaya we can keep you guys covered."

"Where do we go now?" Carlos said.

Stiletto looked out the windows. They were driving fast, putting distance between them and the safe house, but with no destination in mind. Stiletto leaned close to the driver and asked for the radio. The driver handed him the handset. Scott called Majors in the other vehicle.

"We have a plan but we need a place to lay low," Stiletto said.

"I'm open to suggestions."

Back to the Blue Ridge sight seemed safe enough, but it meant getting Fleming involved. Stiletto's gut told him the best way to handle the problem was to act on his own. Keep the leadership out of the discussion. He could explain later, and if General Ike got mad at him, it wouldn't be the first time.

"We need to get out of DC," Stiletto said. "Is there anywhere you can think of?"

"I got a house in Arlington," Majors said. "We can go there."

"Get the address to my driver and we'll regroup at your place."

Majors agreed and Stiletto handed the driver the radio.

Stiletto sat back. The Guardados regarded him without saying anything, but he knew what was on their mind. The same thing he had on his mind. How do they get to Nevada?

CHAPTER THIRTY-SEVEN

Majors had to admit he was a lousy host. He had so little food or beverages in his refrigerator he didn't have much to share with his sudden guests. "The hazards of never being home," he said. But he had a nice two-story home and it was clean. Everybody took the condition of the fridge in stride as he put together what he could, a plate of cold cuts, half a loaf of bread, and a selection of half-empty condiments. Stiletto paced in the living room, thinking, while Majors took care of the refreshments. He wasn't hungry despite the action; he was mad.

Despite the assurances of Robert Mason, the plan had been compromised and their efforts worthless. He didn't see why he shouldn't trust Mason, but until the G-man cleaned the house, there was no further reason to trust the Feds.

Stiletto paced and looked around the room. Majors did not have the usual big screen television on the wall, but instead a small set in a corner. What occupied the walls was a pair of very nice paintings. Stiletto figured

Majors was more interested in the artwork than the latest episodes of *Law & Order*.

When Majors came to Stiletto with a hot mug of tea, he said, "What's on your mind?"

"We have to tell the General."

"I thought we'd decided not to."

"The drivers won't keep their mouths shut. He'll find out one way or another. We can't do this by ourselves either. The more I think about it, the more I know we need help."

"Do you want to call him or shall I?"

"I will make the call," Stiletto said. "If he gives us any heat, it's better if I take it."

"Fair enough."

Stiletto sipped the hot tea. It wasn't Earl Grey, his favorite, but it tasted good. "Thanks for the elixir," he said.

"Good luck with the General." Majors returned to the kitchen where Amaya and the Guardados sat.

Stiletto opened the sliding glass door to the patio and stepped outside. He dialed Fleming on his cell and waited for the boss to answer.

"Scott?" The General sounded panicked.

"We're okay, sir." He explained what happened at the FBI safe house, or, as he called it, the "unsafe house" and Fleming listened without comment. When Scott finished, the General paused before replying. Stiletto swallowed another sip of tea. Majors had let the tea bag steep longer than four minutes; the brew was very strong indeed.

"Sounds like we are up against the wall," Fleming said.

"I agree, sir. But letting them go their own way may be the only option we have now."

"We'll still need to take care of Ramirez and Sanchez. You can bet they won't stop looking; what happened at the safe house had to originate with them, even if the plan leaked."

"If nothing else, getting rid of Ramirez and Sanchez will give Carlos and Jackeline time to go dark."

"We'll sort out those two later," the General said. "Right now, we need to focus on the Guardados. So Nevada, you say?"

"I don't have the exact location, but yes. We're going to need help getting there. Can you arrange quiet transportation?"

"Our usual air resources should be up to scratch. I'll make the calls. Don't tell me where you are. I'll get back with you when it's time. Do you have transport to an airport?"

Stiletto hadn't thought to ask Majors about his personal vehicle. "We'll figure something out, sir."

"Stand by for my call back. Keep your head down."

The General hung up. Stiletto drank some more tea. It had cooled during the conversation. He looked through the kitchen window at the Guardados and Amaya as they ate at the kitchen table. Mike Majors stood to one side using a hand to catch the crumbs from his sandwich. Everybody looked worn out and tired. Too tired to get any sleep, he thought. Stiletto had promised them safe passage; others had broken his promise, and now he needed to help another way.

He went back inside and explained the situation, and suggested everybody try and get a nap before they took off for the next stage. He asked Majors about his car; luckily, The Trust operative owned a minivan, kept in the garage, which would prove useful for their crew.

Stiletto finally took a chair in the living room. The

soft seat gave his tense body immediate relief. He had no idea how they'd resolve the current crisis, but he hoped the only dead bodies would belong to their enemies should they show up in force.

———

Fleming didn't call back till the next morning with flight details. Majors had made a grocery run so at least he could prepare a proper breakfast, and some of the VIPs managed to sleep. Scott noted they looked all right after a decent rest. He was feeling better too, and when he told them a private jet awaited them at Dulles, everybody's mood brightened.

But they were excited to finally leave. Majors drove the minivan. Stiletto felt naked with only his pistol, but Majors had opened a gun safe to hand out semi-auto Colt AR rifles to him and Amaya.

Majors also brought his personal laptop. Once in the air, Jackeline used the plane's Wi-Fi and a Google map to show them where in Nevada she'd hidden her box of gold. It wasn't a big box, she explained, two men could carry it, and it contained only enough gold for around one million bucks. Stiletto noted she said "only" and wanted to laugh. She said they'd be going into the mountains outside Reno. South of Silver Lake off Highway 395. She described the area as dry, filled with brush, but it wasn't like they were going up Mount Everest. It would be an easy hike to and from, though the hike back, carrying the gold, might take a little longer.

"Can we get there by driving?" Stiletto asked.

"I drove," Jackeline explained. "A helicopter would be best, if you can get one."

"We can charter a flight, sure."

"Is that a good idea, Scott?" Amaya said. "You never know who the cartel has hanging around."

"You can say the same thing for renting a car," Stiletto pointed out. "I think we're far enough away from DC where we can operate a little more openly. And they don't have to know Carlos and Jackeline are the passengers."

"If we drive it only takes longer," Jackeline said. "Maybe a chopper is worth the risk if we can get the job done faster."

"What about equipment?" Majors asked.

"We can get shovels and others tools when we land," Stiletto said. "I'm sure they have a Home Depot or something close by."

"We should find a local store," Majors said. "Always shop local. Forget the big chain stores. They're killing small businesses."

"Then we'll shop local," Stiletto said. "Can you zoom in a little more on the spot, Jackeline?"

She did.

The flight continued.

CHAPTER THIRTY-EIGHT

The phone call came around two in the afternoon.

It rang in a small office in the hanger of Baxter Charter at the Reno Airport. Sitting at his desk going over fuel bills, Harvey Baxter set the paperwork down with a sigh and answered the phone. He was happy for the interruption. The rising cost of filling choppers with gasoline was putting a major hole in the small company's bottom line.

"Baxter Charter." He listened to the caller. "Yeah, we can get you a chopper. Where you going?"

He made a face as he listened further. The caller wanted to fly to a spot in the mountains outside of Reno to go on a...treasure hunt?

"You buy a map in a bar or something, sir?"

The caller explained a little more about the trip and said they were willing to pay the required fee for the flight. All the pilot would have to do is get them to the spot and fly them back. He'd have to wait while they tried to dig up the prize, of course.

"Of course," Baxter agreed. "Well, it won't be a problem. How many people do you expect to have in your group?"

The caller gave him the number of passengers involved.

"Sounds fine. When do you want to go? Yeah, we can do today. How does four o'clock sound? Great. We'll have the helicopter gassed up and ready for you at four. What's your name?" Baxter grabbed a pen and scribbled the caller's information on a sheet of scratch paper. He'd have his co-worker, who was the chopper pilot, do the appropriate billing. He thought the story was crazy, so he wanted to wait for the party to arrive before processing the payment.

Baxter said good bye and hung up. He took the scratch paper with its information to the adjoining office. He laughed a little.

"What's so funny?" said Archer Knox. The pilot sat behind a cluttered desk of his own dealing with maintenance invoices.

Knox was the thinner of the two, with Baxter more to the husky and round side. He owned the company, and their office was a small portable building within a hangar with three helicopters inside.

Baxter explained the call.

"Well, if they show up," Knox said, "I'll fly 'em. We need the money. Plus, it will be a good story to tell."

"*If* they show up," Baxter said. He handed Knox the sheet of scratch paper. "I think it's a prank."

"We'll know in a little bit, won't we?"

The clients showed up promptly at four. They entered the hangar, looked around, and started for the office. Baxter saw them through his window and went out to greet them.

Two men and a woman. One of the men was shorter

than his two companions and seemed close to the woman. When he saw their wedding bands, he knew for sure. The woman was a looker too, and Baxter had to keep his gaze from lingering as he showed them the three helicopters and made suggestions on which one would best serve them. He didn't see any of them carrying a treasure map or digging gear; the tall man, who appeared to be in charge, said they had their shovels and whatnot in the car outside. They selected the chopper with the biggest cargo area behind the rear seat, and Baxter let them go get their gear. When they returned, the married couple loaded the chopper while the tall man followed Baxter into the office to do the paperwork and payment.

It was while the tall man was filling out the billing information that Archer Knox waved Baxter into his office. He had an urgent look on his face. Baxter excused himself and joined Knox in his office. Knox drew him away from the door. He held up his cell phone.

"It's them," he whispered. "It's the people Ramirez told us about."

Baxter frowned and took the cell phone from Knox's hand. He examined the facial photographs side-by-side on the screen. The woman held more interest than the man; Baxter drew his fingers across the screen to zoom in on her face. He'd looked at the woman out in the hanger long enough to know Knox was right. Somehow, some way, Carlos and Jackeline Guardado were in his hanger to rent one of his choppers. And based on the alert sent out from Colombia, Baxter realized the "silly" treasure hunt story had a deeper foot in reality than he first gave it credit for.

Running a charter service was no way to get rich, or even, sometimes, keep the rent paid. Now and then they did other jobs on the side, flying packages here and there at the request of a gentleman named Xavier, who worked for certain people in Colombia and paid well for services and discretion. Xavier had promised a significant amount of money should they come in contact with two individuals in whom Xavier's boss had an interest. They knew what they had to do.

"Get them where they want to go," Baxter said, "and stay cool. I'll call this in and let you-know-who do the rest."

"Copy that, boss."

————

Stiletto didn't want to bring Carlos and Jackeline and told them so. He wanted him and Amaya to get the chopper and the gold while Carlos and Jackeline stayed at the hotel with their daughter and Mike Majors. But Jackeline insisted, and he wanted to avoid a fight. Get it done, get it over with; everybody was anxious enough. They didn't need to fight among themselves.

A car was also ruled out at the last moment and a chopper agreed upon; same reason. Speed. Haste. The sooner they grabbed what they needed, the sooner the Guardados could get their new lives started. They were mum on details, but Scott knew if they'd planned ahead with hidden money, they'd planned ahead for other details too.

Stiletto filled out the billing papers and passed them back to the man called Baxter. The boss of the charter service then introduced the pilot, Archer Knox, and he and Stiletto shook hands. Scott followed him out to the hanger where the pilot began inspecting the helicopter, and called for an airport fuel truck to top off the gas tank.

Scott was the only one armed. He had his pistol in the speed rig under his left arm, covered by a light jacket. By the time they were in the air, it was almost five in the evening. They wouldn't have long before the sun started to set, but at least the cooler evening might make the digging a little easier.

CHAPTER THIRTY-NINE

Stiletto watched the ground flash by underneath the chopper. The pilot flew low over the hills.

They'd crossed over Highway 395 a few minutes earlier, and the pilot, Knox, began his descent to about 800 feet above the rolling hills. Jackeline's description had been accurate. The hills were full of dry desert brush, with parallel gouges here and there suggesting regular visits by off-roaders and their vehicles. In the small valleys created by dips between hills, clusters of trees grew in thick patches. Good spots for cover should the need arise.

He glanced at Carlos and Jackeline. They sat beside him with Jackeline in between. Both leaned against Carlos's side of the chopper. She was pointing out the ground to him, speaking into her headset microphone. He followed the conversation over his own headset. They had two channels. One to communicate only with each other, and a second to talk to the pilot. Small electronic boxes connected to the headsets, which they held on their laps, contained the toggle switch. They could leave the pilot out of their conversation, but Stiletto assumed he could eavesdrop if he wanted.

Scott glanced at his phone. He had opened a map app and followed a blue dot representing their movement. The pilot was not deviating from the coordinates Scott had provided before their departure. He didn't know why he remained suspicious, but accepted it was his nature. Being cautious had always served him well, though sometimes the lines between caution and paranoia blurred to where he wasn't sure which was which.

Jackeline pulled away from her husband to lean toward the pilot. She switched channels. Stiletto switched too so he could listen.

"Set us down anywhere you can find a flat area."

"Got one in sight up ahead."

She looked out Stiletto's window in the direction of the valley below. "Okay," she said.

Jackeline switched back to the private channel. "We'll have a short walk but it's not too far."

Stiletto nodded and gave her a thumbs up.

Knox slowed the chopper and hovered over the landing spot a moment. There was no wind to buffet the chopper, so he set the craft down. The rotor wash kicked up a storm of dust. Scott and the Guardados waited till the rotors stopped their rotation before unstrapping seatbelts and climbing out.

They unloaded their digging gear and a tote bag of miscellaneous items and Stiletto told Knox they wouldn't be long. Knox held up a paperback book and said he'd be waiting. "Hope the treasure map you got in the bar works, dude," Knox said. Stiletto laughed. He followed the Guardados as they started off across the dry terrain.

It was warm with clear blue sky. Stiletto checked his

watch. They had maybe forty-five minutes before sunset, but with nothing around them to interfere with the light, they'd have a little more sun to work with. Carlos and Jackeline held the shovels so Stiletto's hands remained free to go for his gun if needed. When they started digging, he'd hand his pistol to her so she could stand watch.

They started up a rise. Jackeline was right. It was an easy hike. As they started down the other side, she directed them to the cluster of trees ahead. They reached the trees and she looked around, walking a circuit around an open spot.

"My marker is gone," she said.

"Blown away by the wind?" Carlos said.

"Does it matter?"

"All right," Stiletto said, "let's start digging in a pattern. Where do you *think* it is, Jackeline?"

She grabbed a fallen branch and drew a box on the ground. "This should be about where it is. Maybe four feet down. Metal box with a handle on top and both sides."

Scott traded her his gun for her shovel. She stepped into the shade while both men sank their shovels into the dirt. The ground was soft and the shovels went in easy, but while four feet wasn't six, Scott knew they still had a long way to go and it wouldn't be easy getting there.

Scott and Carlos built piles of dirt behind them, taking it slow, not wanting to waste energy going too fast. Their supplies included water, and they took breaks every half hour. A chill swept the hills as the sun went down, and when they finally lost the majority of the sun, Jackeline used a flashlight to illuminate the dig.

Stiletto's arms and lower back began to get sore.

When they stopped again for water, he and Carlos agreed they'd dug about three feet. Sweat soaked their shirts and trickled down their faces. The chill helped a little, and what they really needed was a gust of wind to go along with the chill.

Stiletto and Carlos finished their water and resumed digging. They moved a bit faster now since they were nearing the end. Carlos hit the metal box first. They dug further, removing dirt from all sides of the box, until they had the top portion exposed. It was still too deep to pull from the earth. They kept at it.

"It's a little more than four feet, sweetie," Carlos said. He grinned at his wife. She offered only an exaggerated shrug in return.

Stiletto stopped, turning his head left, to listen for a sound he heard. Carlos heard it too, and gave Scott an alarmed look.

Jackeline said, "Is that another chopper?"

"Sounds like it," Stiletto said.

The whipping rotor blades were faint, but grew in volume by the second.

Carlos said, "Might be nothing. Civilian flight heading for—"

"I'm not counting on it, Carlos," Stiletto said. "Get into the trees. Take the shovels."

They hurried into the tree cover, staying close to the thin trunks and watching the sky. Jackeline held the .45 pistol at the ready, but Scott wondered idly what she planned to shoot at. But old habits were old habits.

The incoming chopper flew low over the dig sight, the pilot swinging it around while a man in the passenger seat used binoculars to scan the ground.

"We've been ratted out," Stiletto said. He again traded

Jackeline shovel for gun and told the pair to get back behind better cover than they had at the moment.

They hurried away, stomping over dry brush and leaves. Stiletto dropped to one knee and looked at his .45. He had the pistol and two spare ten-round magazines. He wished they'd brought one of the AR rifles Majors had pulled from his safe. *You play the hand you're dealt.*

The rotor blast from the chopper rustled the trees; when the pilot rotated the helicopter so the side faced him, Stiletto raised the .45 in a two-hand grip. The side door swung open. A man on the seat in the cabin opened fire with a submachine gun, and a swarm of slugs cut into the tree branches, knocking debris down around Scott. He heard no screams from Jackeline or Carlos; a small consolation as he saw more men in the chopper's cabin probably armed with similar weapons to the door gunner.

Stiletto fired three times. The door gunner recoiled as one of the .45 slugs struck. The other two smacked into the side of the enemy chopper. The pilot tilted the nose forward and flew out of Scott's line of fire. But now they'd land and unload the remaining shooters.

Stiletto broke left, weaving through the wooded patch to drop on his belly at the edge of the tree line. The chopper touched down about fifty yards away. Too far for a .45 to be any good, but they didn't know what else he and the Guardados had. *Joke's on them.* But Stiletto figured there was still a way to try and better the odds.

A branch snapped behind him. He whirled around to see Carlos join him. Scott gave him the update. "You and your wife scoot. Avoid Knox. I think he's the rat."

"How?"

"You can bet I'll ask him. Go. If I make it, I'll come looking for you. Go!"

Carlos ran back to his wife. Stiletto silently wished them Godspeed. They were woefully unprepared and outgunned; time to try and create an advantage.

Stiletto left the tree line and stayed low as he followed a diagonal slope, dropping to his belly to crawl within a batch of dry brush. Lousy cover; decent concealment. From his raised position he saw the enemy chopper and counted four shooters. One, the wounded door gunner, remained in the chopper. He figured the man in the passenger seat with the binoculars joined the fight as the fourth shooter, but Scott failed to identify him as the gunners advanced. He'd be the man in charge. He buttoned out the partially spent mag, and replaced it with one of his spare ten-round mags. With an extra cartridge in the chamber, he had eleven shots. *Use them well.*

The gunners approached at a fast clip, spreading out, trying to stay low, but the lack of cover left them exposed. The lack of cover didn't help Scott either. The only advantage the enemy had was firepower; Stiletto had surprise, and hoped it was enough.

He waited. The gunners moved closer. The fading light might help, he realized, and then they were within ten yards. He held his fire and didn't move. If they didn't see him until it was too late, he might get them all.

Five yards. The gunners came up on Stiletto's right, following a path through a gap between the hill Stiletto rested on and the one across from him. When they had passed and increased speed for the trees, Stiletto turned around, rose into a crouch, and opened fire.

He started with the last man first. The .45 slug hit the man in the neck above his shoulder blades. He fell without a sound, and his comrades dropped to shoot at the trees. They fired short bursts to conserve ammo, and Stiletto moved closer. Another shot brought down a second gunner; a double-tap took out a third as he got smart and turned his head. The last man, who followed his buddy's action, turned to face Scott and bring up his SMG at the same time. Stiletto fired first. Both rounds ripped into the last man's chest, bringing him down in a growing pool of blood mixed with dirt to form a reddish muck.

Stiletto lowered his gun but didn't slow down. He ran to the fallen shooters, grabbed a submachine gun, and turned and run after the chopper. But he was too late. The chopper was already taking off and flying away, and there was nobody left to question except Archer Knox and his boss. Stiletto slung the sub gun, helped himself to a few spare magazines as well as a second weapon, and went looking for Carlos and Jackeline.

They had to deal with Knox first. If the pilot expected a signal from his buddies, he had a long wait coming.

———

They found Knox at the chopper, not reading his book as advertised but instead pacing nervously. When he saw Stiletto, Carlos, and Jackeline and their weapons, he froze. Scott aimed his sub gun at the pilot and said, "Hold it, Knox."

"You got the gun, dude. Listen, I can—"

Stiletto swung the SMG and hit Knox in the belly. The pilot went down, gasping. He grimaced as Stiletto knelt beside him with a knee in his belly. His eyes darted to Carlos and Jackeline, who moved behind Scott, then shifted back to Stiletto.

"You can explain?" Scott said. "Start."

Knox took only five minutes to tell them about his and Baxter's connection to the drug trade, their buddy Xavier, who led the team from the chopper, and how they had wanted to collect the reward money for the capture of Carlos and Jackeline Guardado.

Stiletto stood up once the pilot finished speaking. He turned to his companions. "We can't shoot him unless one of you knows how to fly a helicopter."

Carlos and Jackeline admitted they could not fly a helicopter.

"Then let's find something to tie him with and go finish our business."

They did.

CHAPTER FORTY

General Ike said, "The two men from the helicopter company are in custody."

"Good," Stiletto said. He sat in his usual chair in front of Fleming's desk. Beyond the office, in the Pit, the Trust's support personnel busied themselves with activities supporting ongoing missions elsewhere in the world.

"The whole matter has left us with a mess to clean up. The FBI isn't happy."

"I'm not concerned about the FBI right now, General. Don't tell me about a mess. They have one of their own, and it's huge. Worse than we realized. They need to get their own house clean before they complain about us."

"I agree."

"Has it upset any of the plans for future cooperation you had?"

"Cooperation with the federal government is the last thing The Trust needs, Scott. It was never the goal. We might like some consideration now and then, an acknowledgment of existence, but we never wanted to join forces. It's the antithesis of what Number One and his partners started out to accomplish."

Stiletto nodded.

"But the job is done. Did Carlos and Jackeline give you any clue where they might go?"

"None, and I didn't ask. We said our good byes and that was the end."

"Well, at least they are safe, and we have their information. May they never again return to their former activities."

"It bothers me they might," Stiletto said. "How many other bad guys have been given second chances only to pick up where they left off?"

"I'm sure we can think of a few," Fleming said. "I wouldn't dwell on it. Because if they do—"

"I'll see them again, yeah."

"I don't have anything more for you right now. Any other plans?"

"I have an appointment with Dr. Gargarin. Follow-up."

"Good luck."

Stiletto rose from the chair. He zipped up his jacket. "Thank you, sir. I'll be at home tonight if you need me."

Fleming smiled. "One never knows what might come up. Get some rest."

"Yes, sir." Stiletto started for the office.

"One more thing, Scott."

Stiletto paused, turned around.

"We have some loose ends. Ramirez and Sanchez. Any ideas?"

"I could go back and visit."

"You've done enough."

"Maybe get David at CIA to repay the favor he owes you."

"And how might he do so?"

"Send our love via drone strike." Stiletto winked. He opened the office door and departed.

Fleming waited for the door to click shut before reaching for his telephone. *Great minds think alike.* Fleming had thought of a similar solution earlier in the morning.

He dialed David McNeil at CIA and waited for the connection to go through. McNeil answered the direct line.

"It's Ike," Fleming said. "I wonder if you can help us out with something in Colombia. Put a bow on the recent mission, if you like."

The two men talked for fifteen minutes.

————

Stiletto eased into the chair in the doctor's office.

"You look tired," Dr. Gargarin said. He occupied his usual seat minus the notepad this time. Stiletto wondered if it was of any significance.

"I'm tired and sore all over," Stiletto said. "Last mission was a bear and I never want to do this again."

"Do you mean that?"

"Not really, but hopefully it will be a while before the next one. My old bones need a break."

"Can you tell me about it?"

"A little." Stiletto gave him the bare minimum without mentioning names or too much detail. "It was a mission in Colombia to get informants out. We had more trouble than we figured we would. There was a young girl involved, our informant's daughter, so I had a personal investment in the job whether I wanted to admit it or not. And I didn't."

"Why not?"

"Because normally these people would be enemies. But they'd turned to help our side. It took me a while to accept they were walking away from their old life, but eventually I did. I actually grew quite fond of them."

"Did you get them out?" the doctor said.

"We did. They're safe. And hopefully on their way to a better life where they don't have to worry about people trying to kill them."

"Dangerous times, isn't it?"

"When hasn't it been?" Stiletto said. "I remember growing up and listening to my father and his army buddies talk about going to war with the Russians. Here we are thirty years later still talking about going to war with other nations. Nothing ever changes except the names on the map."

"But you keep fighting."

"I do."

"Why?"

"Because I can."

"You mentioned that as a motivator in our first session," Dr. Gargarin said. "Does it ever feel hollow to you?"

"Meaningless?"

"Sure."

"Sometimes. But then I have a beer and take a nap and usually want to get back into the fight."

"I know a guy who was in your line of work too," Dr. Gargarin said. "He's in his sixties now. His body is pretty banged up and he's on pain killers for various injuries. He'd do it all over again despite the consequences he's living with now."

"We're all crazy, aren't we?" Stiletto said. "We have to be, I guess."

"You're men with a different state of mind than average. I think we need people like you."

Stiletto nodded. He wasn't sure where the doctor was going with his line of conversation, but he decided not to argue and let it follow its natural course.

"We talked about your daughter last time. Felicia, right?"

Stiletto nodded again.

"You had said you weren't sure she was still alive or needed money or anything like that. Do you realize you have resources at your disposal to check on her? Quietly, I mean. She wouldn't have to know you're, you know, spying on her."

"I do."

"Why haven't you used them?"

"I signed agreements saying I wouldn't abuse those resources. Checking up on my daughter, even if my boss said it was okay, wouldn't be right. Wouldn't be *legal*, either."

"But if you were really worried—"

"I suppose I could bend the rules. They've never stopped me before, in other things. But maybe I'm not willing to bend this particular one. I want her to come back when she's ready. Violating her privacy, even if she never knew, sort of works against that desire."

"You're afraid of driving her away for good."

"It might already be too late, Doctor."

"You never told me your wife's name."

"It's in my file."

"Right. You mentioned your informants had a daughter. Was she the same age as yours?"

"No, still a teenager."

"I see. Did helping keep this family together give you any solace over your own situation?"

"I'm not sure I make the connection."

"How did it feel to help this family?"

"Pretty good."

"How do you see this situation relating to your own life?"

Stiletto paused while he considered his answer.

"A little angry," he said.

"Why?"

"It's the constant battle, Doctor. I can help others, but I'm not very good at helping myself."

"Most people aren't. We're too close to our own problems. We have mental blocks we don't want to face getting in the way of solutions."

"You're leading to something, aren't you?"

"What was your wife's name?"

"I've told you it's in my *file*, Doctor."

"You came to me because you said not talking about your problems is becoming a problem, remember?"

"I do."

"If we're going to get beyond the mental blocks you don't realize you have, we need to ask tough questions, and you need to answer them."

Stiletto felt his heart rate increase. He shifted in the chair.

"In other words," the doctor said, "I can't help you until you're ready to help yourself. You have to break the barriers, Scott."

Stiletto said nothing. He breathed steady to keep calm.

"You've come through a very tough, very stressful situation," Gargarin said. "Why is it harder to tell me your wife's name?"

"Lose yours and *then* ask me."

"You and my sixty-year-old friend have the ability to

do amazing things most people would be too frightened to try. You can tell me your wife's name. No violence required. All you have to do is talk. Break down the barrier, Scott."

"How?" Scott almost whispered the word. He felt confidence leaving him. His voice shook as he continued. "What am I supposed to do?"

"Tell me your wife's name."

Stiletto shifted his eyes away from the doctor and stared at the carpet. He breathed deep. His heart rate was up, he felt nervous, felt his body shaking as he fought back tears.

"What was her name?"

Gargarin asked the question softly this time. Stiletto's vision blurred as his eyes teared up.

"Maggie," he said, and finally broke. He sobbed, and wiped his eyes with his left hand. He reached for the box of tissues on the table beside the chair.

"Her name was Maggie," he said.

CHAPTER FORTY-ONE

Jorge Ramirez of the northern branch of Colombia's Beltran-Leyva Cartel stepped out of the limousine and buttoned his coat as he surveyed the circular driveway and the large number of armed men stationed about. Movement on the roof caught his attention. He looked up. A man with binoculars scanned the clear blue sky.

Fausto Sanchez met Ramirez at the top of the steps between marble columns and they entered the mansion.

"What's happening, Fausto?" Ramirez said. They crossed the tiled floor.

"I can't reach our people in America."

"It means they failed."

"Then the Guardados are forever out of our reach," Sanchez said. "What do we do now?"

"What we've always done. Survive."

They stepped out on the rear balcony. More armed troops prowled the grounds.

"What's with the man on the roof?" Ramirez said.

"Looking for drones."

The pair sat at a table and one of Sanchez's servants

brought sparkling water. Ramirez wasn't thirsty and let his glass sit.

"I have a plane ready to take me to Nicaragua," Ramirez said. "From there I'll get to my hideout, but what about you?"

"Chopper on the way. Same thing. The Americans may come after us to finish what they started."

Ramirez said, "We may be on the run for some time, Fausto."

Sanchez laughed. He swallowed some of his drink. "But we'll still be in control of our various empires, Jorge."

The man on the roof pointed, yelling.

Sanchez and Ramirez jumped from their seats, looking up as a Hellfire missile fired from a Predator drone zeroed in on the mansion, its white contrail contrasting against the blue sky. Neither man had time to run; fear froze them in place. Running wouldn't have mattered anyway. The rocket smacked into the center of the balcony behind the two men and obliterated them in an explosion so intense it toppled half the mansion and two nearby trees.

The echo of the blast carried through the air.

A LOOK AT: THE KILL FEVER

A Sam Raven Thriller

SAM RAVEN TRIES TO GET AWAY FROM HIS WAR WITHOUT END, BUT CONFLICT FINDS HIM AGAIN IN THIS EMOTIONAL ROLLER-COASTER THRILLER BY THE AUTHOR OF *THE DANGEROUS MR. WOLF*.

Sam Raven, a man with a mysterious past, finds himself in harm's way when he saves the life of a woman running from a trio of killers. She's a thief named Megan, and her latest score has drawn the attention of every cut-throat looking for a fast buck, and an intelligence community out to protect a secret at any cost--including murder.

They don't trust each other, but Megan knows Raven is her only chance to survive. As he uses every skill in his arsenal, their enemies get closer, and this time victory isn't assured. Only a desperate last battle will determine who walks away.

AVAILABLE NOW